MW01518562

A
CHRISTMAS
HOMETOWN
REUNION

By

S. I. WELLS

For permission to reproduce selections from this book, write to: info@staythirstymedia.com – Atten: Permissions.

ISBN: 979-8-218-31512-2

THE HOLIDAY SERIES

An Imprint of Stay Thirsty Publishing

A Division of

STAY THIRSTY MEDIA, INC.

staythirstypublishing.com

For

Mrs. Wells

The true love of my life.
Who signed up for the ride and has been by my side ever since.
She is my rock and the supplier of love, encouragement
and fresh horses when the wind is in our faces.

A CHRISTMAS HOMETOWN REUNION

By

S. I. WELLS

CHAPTER 1

It was late when Ben Wallace arrived at his apartment after an exhausting day at work and listened to the voicemail his mother had left earlier in the day:

"Hi Honey, it's Mom. You know Christmas is almost here and we know how hard you have been working at your law firm and that you can't get away to come home. So, your father and I decided that we will bring the entire family up to Chicago and stay with you! It will be a Christmas Hometown Reunion! You haven't seen your sisters and everyone in almost three years. We are even bringing Sara to watch the grandkids and driving all the way from Iowa in your father's new RV. And we have two new puppies! Doesn't that sound grand?"

Panic overtook Ben and he began to hyperventilate. He loved his family, but "mom's plan" had the hallmark of nightmare written all over it.

He grabbed a beer from the refrigerator and started to catalog the reasons mom and dad's idea just couldn't work:

First, he was in the middle of closing the make-or-break deal of his legal career. If he managed to pull it through to conclusion, he had a very good chance of making partner early next year.

Second, where was he going to put everyone? He was a subtenant in a Fulton Market loft, which was pretty large, but the two girls who were the principal tenants were probably going to freak out because they lived there full-time too.

Third, how was he going to explain to his very conservative Iowa farm family that his roommates were a lesbian couple. And fourth, Sara was his high school girlfriend, who he hadn't seen for nearly ten years, and he was currently in a very serious relationship with Gillian for the past six months. Nothing good could come from their meeting.

At that moment, Ben's roommates, Mackenzie and Siobhan, returned from a date-night dinner together. They were slightly intoxicated, bumping into each other and laughing at some private joke.

He had met Siobhan through his law firm. She was the Vice President of a very large private equity fund and Mackenzie was finishing up her MD at the University of Chicago. Both were smart, tough and driven in their own way. He loved the loft and considered himself fortunate to have found this living arrangement but was nervous about how they would take the soon-to-arrive Wallace family circus.

"Ladies," Ben began, gathering up his courage, "I have something to discuss. Do you have a few minutes?"

CHAPTER 2

Ben gestured to Mackenzie and Siobhan to take a seat on the living room couch just opposite from his favorite reading chair.

"I realize this will come as a surprise to you, and it certainly did to me, but my entire family is driving from Iowa to Chicago for Christmas and my mom announced they are staying with me."

Ben paused and grimaced, waiting for their reaction.

Siobhan took the lead.

"Ben, you know we love having you as a roomie. You are a great guy. You keep to yourself, and you respect our privacy. However, ... the answer is no."

Mackenzie nodded her agreement.

Ben was prepared.

"I was pretty sure that was going to be your response. Frankly that was my first response to my family's plan. But they are on the road, and I'm stuck."

Siobhan sat stone-faced.

"So, I have an idea," Ben continued. "While my family visits, why don't I arrange for you to stay at a very nice downtown hotel for a week, all expenses on me? Think of it like a surprise vacation!"

Without missing a beat, Siobhan replied, "Why not put your family up in the hotel and they can have a very nice vacation?"

"You don't understand, my family are very plain, Iowa apple

farming people, no frills, family first, salt of the earth, you know ..."

Ben took a deep breath.

"If I even offered, they would be deeply hurt. I can't do that to them."

"Ben, you know my hospital schedule," Mackenzie said. "I am on 24- and 48-hour shifts. When I come home, I am exhausted and peace and quiet is the only thing that gives me a chance to recharge."

"Consider the matter settled," Siobhan added. "You will just have to find another way to fix this."

Just as Ben was about to try to appeal their decision, the front door app on his phone lit up.

"Hi Ben, it's Gillian. Surprise!"

CHAPTER 3

Gillian Clark was an Ivy-League preppy type, smart, ambitious and overly anxious to be somebody that everyone noticed. When she walked into the living room of the apartment, Mackenzie and Siobhan immediately excused themselves. They were not fans.

"Gillian, what a nice surprise!" Ben kissed her hello. "I have some exciting news."

"Do tell." Gillian took his hand and led him to the couch where she curled up very close to him.

"I received a voicemail from my mom and my family is driving from Iowa to spend Christmas with me! Isn't that great?"

Gillian wasn't sure. "Uh-huh. What does that exactly mean?"

"Well," Ben replied slowly, as he worked out the details in his mind, "I guess they will be up here in Chicago ... like tourists and will want me to show them around and be with them ... all the time."

"But what about our Christmas plans, just you and me, and the people who are expecting to see us?"

"Sure, I understand, but I think we will have to play it by ear. Look, I told you about my family. They are backcountry folks. Unsophisticated, but well-meaning. I don't come from much, but they have supported me for my whole life, and I wouldn't do anything to disappoint them."

"I get that, but what about me? People are depending on seeing me, with you, during the holidays. We have places to go and people to see. Can't you explain *that* to your family? I'm sure they would understand."

Ben felt his chest muscles tightening from stress.

"Look, Ben, you are going to have to make a decision sooner or later. It's your life in Chicago, where the world could be at your feet ... or your life in Backwater, Iowa. You know how I feel about you and how I see us ascending to the heights of Chicago society as a young, devastatingly good-looking couple. I don't mean to put pressure on you," she continued, "but now is the time when you have to separate from your past and become someone important."

"Gillian, you've made your point. I've had a really exhausting day. Can we continue this conversation tomorrow? Let me drive you home."

"No need, I'll Uber so you can think it over. I won't wait long."

CHAPTER 4

The next morning, Ben's phone rang at 6:30am, jolting him awake. The Caller ID read: MOM.

"Hi, Honey, this is your mom. I'm glad to get you on the phone. I hope I didn't wake you. I just wanted to let you know our schedule. We are making a slight detour to Springfield, you know in Southern Illinois, to visit your Aunt Katherine. She just took some kind of new job doing something at a courthouse."

"When do you expect to arrive in Chicago?" Ben asked, as he wiped the sleep from his eyes.

"Well, it looks like we will be there in two days from now. As I told you in my message, your dad bought a new RV and there is enough room for everyone. Your sisters are excited to see you and the grans are just excited to be on a trip with our two new beagle puppies. You are going to love them –we named them Hill and Dale. They are so lively and fun."

Ben shook his head at his coming "good fortune."

"Now, Honey, your dad gave me very clear instructions to tell you to find a place for him to park the RV, and also to buy a bunch of blow-up air mattress beds with blankets, sheets and pillows. We want everyone to be comfortable because it doesn't sound like you have enough bedrooms in your apartment. Dad said to go on Amazon and order everything. He will reimburse you when we arrive."

"How many are you again?"

"Well, it's me and your dad, your sister Catlin – she is still unmarried you know – your sister Holly and her husand Todd, their kids, Billy and Lily, and we brought Sara Holcolm, you remember her from high school, well, she is a teacher now on Christmas break, to take care of the kids and the dogs. So, I guess that is eight. Won't this be fun!"

"OK, Mom, I got it. Say hello to Aunt Katherine for me."

Ben hung up and rolled over to scream into his pillow. He had no idea how he was going to make this work out.

His phone rang again. The Caller ID read: NED MARTIN. He was one of the senior partners at the law firm of Martin & Martin where he worked.

CHAPTER 5

"Wallace," Ned Martin began, "where are you?"

"At my apartment, Sir. It's not even 7 yet."

"I know what time it is. You'd better get your butt into the office in a hurry. I just received a call that your merger deal with the Westwoods started to fall apart last night. Do you know why?"

"First I've heard of it," Ben replied as his muscles started to tense up again.

"Look, it's not my job, it's your job, but whatever it is, you need to fix this. Your future at this firm depends on it."

"Yes, Sir, I understand."

"I set up a Zoom call with the Westwoods for 8am this morning for you. So, get in here and figure this out!"

Ben wanted to pull the covers over his head or just crawl in a hole, but he realized he didn't have the time or the luxury. He knew if he pulled this deal over the finish line, he would be eligible to make partner sometime next year.

Just as he was toweling himself dry after a quick shower, his bathroom door swung open. Mackenzie stood in the doorway crying.

"No knock?"

"Ben, I'm sorry, but I have to talk to someone."

"Look, you go sit on my bed and we can talk while I get dressed. I've been called into the firm on an emergency."

Two minutes later, wearing just his boxers, he emerged

from the bathroom to finishing getting dressed.
"OK, Mac, let me have it. What's going on?"

CHAPTER 6

"Siobhan and I had a really bad fight last night," Mackenzie told Ben, in between her tears.

"Fights do happen," Ben replied, as he continued to get dressed for work.

"This one was different. She was very mean to me. She tore into me and said I was too stupid to be a good doctor, and that I should just give up and be a pretty housewife."

"Now that's harsh," Ben said, as he buttoned his shirt and slid into his suit trousers.

"Harsh? She thinks she is the smartest person on the planet and everyone else is stupid. What gives her the right to treat me like that?"

Mackenzie stopped talking as her sobs overtook her whole body.

Ben sat on the bed next to her. He held her in his arms to comfort her.

"Look," he said, "sometimes people say things they don't mean; that they will regret later. Here you are at the top of your med school class, on your way to becoming a surgeon, and you are letting yourself get sucked into her anger. I can't say what's on Siobhan's mind, but you just need to step back and realize who you are, what your value is and how much you have achieved. I realize that love does blind people from reason, but you can overcome this."

Mackenzie looked at him. "Thank you."

With the storm beginning to pass, Ben went to find a tie

and finish getting dressed.

"I hope you don't think me ungrateful," Mackenzie said, "but I think I need to have my own space. Siobhan and I talked about it, and we think maybe you should move out so that I can have your room."

"You know, heat of the moment thinking," he replied off-handedly, as he put on his suit jacket, although he felt his blood pressure rising.

"No, we kind of made up our minds last night. You know with your family coming and all. Then we had a fight. So, will you?"

"Sure ... sure," Ben answered, "but first I have to get to my office. My deal is imploding, and I have a Zoom with my clients in twenty minutes."

CHAPTER 7

Ben reached his desk with only five minutes to spare before his Zoom with Betty and Arnold Westwood. They had been his clients for the better part of a year. He thought they were wonderful people; down-to-earth, honest and sincere, much like his own parents.

Betty was the CEO of their tech company, B-A-W Innovations, named for "Betty-Arnold-Westwood." She had a Bachelor's Degree in Computer Science and a Master's Degree in Quantum Mechanics from Cal Tech and a Ph.D. in Nanotechnology from MIT, but you would never know it from her soft, grandmotherly manner with neatly coiffed grey hair. What gave her away were her piercing, ice-blue eyes that reflected a first-rate intellect.

Arnold, on the other hand, was an inventor/absentminded professor type with a Ph.D. from MIT in Renewable Energy and Nanotechnology. He was on the Autism/Asperger's spectrum that Betty concluded was responsible for his genius.

They met at MIT while earning their respective Ph.D.s, and fell into an easy, trusting relationship. They shared a love of discovery, for walking into the scientific unknown and for challenging Mother Nature whenever they could. They had an awkward courtship for two years that bloomed into marriage one afternoon before a Justice of the Peace over thirty years ago.

They had no children, because Betty could not, and they

devoted their lives to each other and their work. When Betty had the idea to start their business, it was her parents that loaned them the initial funds to form B-A-W Innovations. Over the decades, the company grew slowly, in part because Betty would not take on loans or outside partners. She prized their independence and steered the company through the fat and lean times.

Arnold held dozens of patents, but three of his inventions revolutionize the regulation of power in cell phone batteries and electric car engines. His excitement came in the process of invention, and he hardly noticed if any of his inventions had any practical application. He left that up to Betty.

Betty totally understood Arnold, looked out for him and never put pressure on him to do things that he couldn't process.

They lived modestly and to the outside world, they looked like a nice "older couple," but their looks belied their wealth and scientific influence.

"Hi, Betty and Arnold," Ben began the call. "Always nice to see you both. What's going on?"

Betty took the lead.

"Ben, we are concerned that the buyers of our company are trying to put pressure on us to force the purchase price down. They are spreading rumors that our technology isn't as good as it is and that we don't pay our bills on time. Of course, both are completely untrue, as you well know."

"Betty," Ben replied in a calming tone, "this just looks like pre-closing maneuvering. Your buyers are Gen Z'ers and they don't understand that this will come back to haunt them. I'll call their attorney and tell him to get his clients under control. As far as I am concerned, everything is on track to have this deal close on Christmas Eve per the contract."

"We are in your hands," Betty remarked. "We trust you and we know you will do the right thing for us."

"Of course," Ben replied. "You can just go about your day and let me take care of this."

Ben waited for the Westwoods to end the call before he left the Zoom meeting.

"Jessie," Ben shouted to his secretary, whose desk was just on the other side of the wall to his office. "Have we heard anything from Attorney Dunn about the Westwood deal?"

"Nothing," she replied.

Ben pulled out his cell phone and dialed Charles Dunn at his office. The call was bounced to a voicemail.

Before he could leave a message, Neil Martin, the other senior partner of Martin & Martin burst into his office.

"My brother told me that the Westwood deal is about to fall apart. The fees from this deal are already factored into the firm's annual calculations. You need to close it on time … if you still want to be considered for partner next year."

"I understand," Ben replied.

With that, Neil Martin abruptly turned and marched out of Ben's office.

Ben dialed Attorney Dunn's cell phone number again. It went to voicemail again.

CHAPTER 8

Anderson Wallace and his wife, Molly, their unmarried 30-year-old daughter Caitlin, their married daughter Holly, with her husband, Todd Swift, their two young children, Billy and Lily, with their temporary nanny, Sara, who was really the Second Grade teacher in the local grammar school, were singing, "The wheels on the bus ... " as the Wallace RV motored down the highway on the family's Christmas reunion tour. Their two new rambunctious beagle pups had joined in to make quite a chorus.

The Wallace's had closed-up the farmhouse, arranged for neighbor McSweeny to feed their small flock of chickens, passel of pigs and herd of three cows while they were gone, and left word with just about everyone in their town of 900 souls that they were going to visit Ben in the big city.

Anderson Wallace was a fifth-generation apple farmer from Wallaceton, Iowa. He grew up on the family farm with two brothers and one sister. His brothers were both drafted into the army during the Vietnam War and were both killed. His sister contracted meningitis at college and passed away after a brief illness.

Anderson was the last descendant of the Wallace clan that originally emigrated to the United States from Scotland in the mid-1800s. He was educated at the local high school in Wallaceton and was accepted into the University of Iowa for college. He fancied himself as a musician in those days and started a three-man banjo band during his freshman year.

Although the band was having some local success, when the movie *Deliverance* was released with the dueling banjo scene people thought banjo music was creepy, and from that point on, their gigs dried up.

Early in his sophomore year at Iowa, his two older brothers died in the war and his parents told him he had to come home to help with the apple farm. Two years later, just after his sister died, his parents were killed when a drunk driver's car hit their truck one night.

From that time on, Anderson was a changed person, feeling the weight of his family's tragedies and the difficulty in keeping the family farm afloat.

Molly Grant grew up three towns west of Wallaceton but did not meet Anderson until they were both freshmen in college at Iowa. At first, she was attracted to him because of his banjo music, and they dated on and off for most of the next year.

Molly's family was middle class but lost its money in a Ponzi scheme when she was halfway through her sophomore year. Her parents were elderly, and she was forced to drop out of college and move back home to tend to them. She had one sister, Katherine, who was older and who had left home for college ten years before Molly was out of high school.

Molly and Anderson lost touch after they returned to their respective homes but bumped into each other by accident at the County hospital one day while Molly was visiting her mother in the hospital and Anderson was hand-delivering bushels of fresh apples to the nursing stations, as the Wallace family had done for over 50 years.

Their courtship lasted nearly five years. Anderson finally proposed to Molly, and they were married at the Wallace family farm. They were 32 years old on their wedding day over 38 years ago.

When the sing-along had run its course, Molly moved her seat to be next to Anderson as he drove.

"I'm worried about Ben," she began. "I think he is under a lot of pressure in this job of his, and I don't think he is working for very nice people."

"Comes with the territory," Anderson replied. "His choice to become a lawyer."

"I hope going to see him doesn't turn out to be a bad idea. I wouldn't want to make it harder on him."

"The sword gains strength with each pass through the fire."

"I know, you always remind me of that, Anderson, but look at the crowd we are bringing with us."

"It's important that he feels part of the family. Wouldn't want him to drift apart. He needs to remember the stock he comes from."

"How long until we reach Springfield?" Molly asked. "I want to let Katherine know."

"About five hours. We should be at the Walmart by four this afternoon."

"At the next rest stop, I think I'll give Ben a call and let him know how excited everyone is to see him ... in just two days!"

CHAPTER 9

Ben was frantically trying to reach Attorney Dunn. He called all three phone numbers on Dunn's email signature with no luck. Three calls and three voicemail messages. He left his own messages and hoped to get a return call within the hour.

Just as he was about to pull out the deal memo for the Westwoods' sale to TECH-AI, his cell phone rang. The Caller ID read: MOM. He pushed the "Decline" button. Now was not the time to talk to her.

His cell rang again. The Caller ID read: GILLIAN. He pushed the "Decline" button, fully aware there would be consequences. In a feeble attempt to lessen the blow, he sent her an "IN MEETING" reply text.

Then he remembered he needed to order air mattresses and bedding. He jumped on Amazon and started searching for things that could be delivered tomorrow. He was quickly overwhelmed by the number of choices and realized this assignment was going to take him more than just a few minutes. And when he saw the prices, he hoped his Mastercard had enough credit remaining to pull this off.

His cell phone rang again. The Caller ID read: MAC-KENZIE. He hit the "Decline" button yet again. That problem would have to wait until tonight.

Ben's secretary poked her head into his office, "Charles Dunn is on Line 1 for you."

He took a deep breath before reaching for his office phone.

CHAPTER 10

"Ben Wallace," Ben announced as he answered Attorney Dunn's call.

"Look, Wallace," Dunn said in a belligerent tone, "what's going on with the Westwoods. Are they trying to screw my clients?"

"I don't know what you are talking about," Ben replied, trying to remain calm.

"The watchdogs at TECH-AI are always on the lookout for what the competition is doing. Yesterday they heard a rumor that a new patent application was being filed that would make the Westwood's technology obsolete. If this is true, you just bought yourself a world of hurt."

"Mr. Dunn, I don't appreciate your tone."

"Wallace, I don't appreciate getting blindsided," Dunn shot back.

Sensing that the conversation was beginning to spin out of control, Ben changed tactics. "As I said, I don't know anything about this, but I will be happy to look into it for you."

"By five today or the deal's off," Dunn bellowed. "If I don't hear from you with a satisfactory response, my clients have authorized me to file a fraud lawsuit tomorrow and demand repayment of all the monies spent setting up this deal and doing the due diligence, along with punitive damages in the millions."

"Mr. Dunn, I will call you back with details, but let the record reflect that I really don't like your attitude," Ben replied as sternly as he could and was glad that Dunn couldn't see how his hands were shaking. "I'll be back to you."

Ben hung up first and felt good about it.

The feeling didn't last long. His cell phone rang. The Caller ID read: MOM.

CHAPTER 11

"Hi, Mom!" Ben answered, trying not to let on about his contentious call with Attorney Dunn.

"Hi, Honey. I can't tell you how excited everyone in the family is to be spending seven days during Christmas with you. It will be so nice to have the entire family together again during the holidays, and in the big city, too!"

In the background, Anderson Wallace's voice could be heard loud and clear. "Molly, tell Ben that we will be arriving in two days, on Wednesday. I figure it will be around 3:30 in the afternoon. He needs to be at his apartment when we arrive, and he needs to show me where to park the RV."

"Did you hear your father?" Molly asked.

"Yes, Mom, I did. Wednesday, 3:30pm, at my apartment, with a place to park dad's RV. No problem."

"Good, Honey, and you might order some groceries to get us started. Your sisters and I can shop when we get there, but it would be nice to have a few things when we arrive."

"Of course," Ben replied. "Anything else?"

"No. Can't wait to see you again!"

No sooner had his call ended that Ben realized he had never completed the air mattress order on Amazon. He decided he would give his bed to his parents, order a full-size mattress for Holly and Todd, singles for Catlin, Billy, Lily and Sara and he would sleep on the couch. He completed the order and Amazon promised to deliver tomorrow night by 8pm.

His brief moment of satisfaction, however, was interrupted by a second call attempt from Gillian.

CHAPTER 12

Gillian was angry.

"Ben, why were you avoiding my call?"

"Gillian ... look ... I told you I'm in the middle of this big deal at the firm and things are not going well. Plus, and I hope you understand, the entire Wallace family circus is about to descend on my apartment. And my roommates want me to move out because they are in and out of lovers' quarrels."

"And that affects me how?" she asked.

Ben wasn't sure how to respond. Luckily, she just kept on talking.

"I have a big surprise. I managed to get us invited to a special dinner held in honor of prospective new members of the Art Institute Junior Board. This is a very big deal. The top of Chicago society will be there, and I was very fortunate to get us included. This is a big step up toward our goal."

"Where and when?"

"At the Art Institute, of course, this coming Thursday night from 6:30 to 10. Oh, it's Black Tie, so you will need a tux. Do you have one?"

Ben just shook his head in response.

"Ben ... is that a *Yes*? If not, you will need to get one right away."

And yet another assignment, he thought to himself.

"I've got to jet. I have an appointment at Saks for a new gown. It's long, it's red and it glitters. We will really stand out."

She abruptly hung up.

Ben was actually glad for the silence. His mind was spinning from all the chaos in his life.

Then he remembered the Westwoods and the demands from the buyer's bad-tempered attorney.

"Jessie," Ben shouted to his secretary, "Please get the Westwoods on the line for me."

CHAPTER 13

"Hi, Ben," Betty Westwood said as she answered his phone call. "How are you doing?"

"Betty," Ben replied, "let me cut to the chase. Your buyers think there is a newly filed patent application out there that is going to totally compromise the technology your company is based on. Their lawyer is a nasty guy who is throwing his weight around with threats of a fraud lawsuit against you for hiding this information and he said they will be asking for millions in damages. If this is true, your deal is hanging by a thread."

Betty started to laugh.

"Oh, Ben, I'm so sorry," she replied, "we have been so busy that we just forgot to mention it. Arnold filed a patent application last week for a quantum chip that will power the next generation of computers. It's years from anyone's ability to use one of these quantum computers, but you know Arnold, he is not restrained by time or reality."

Ben took a long, slow, deep breath.

"And will that patent be included in the sale?" he asked.

"Of course, dear, we want the company to prosper far into the future. We have an interest in that, and we will honor the price we settled on. We would never take advantage of someone or hide something. Our name is on the door. You know us."

"Ben," Arnold said from the background, "you can't stop an old man from making stuff up, and sometimes, it actually works!"

"OK, I'll get to the buyer's attorney and calm everything down. So sorry to bother you both with this, but it is par for the course. There is always some pushing and shoving before a deal closes."

"Ben," Betty said, "you just keep doing the right thing as you always do. That's why we are so fond of you."

When the call ended, Ben picked up his cell phone and dialed Charles Dunn's number, anticipating a lowering of the temperature between them.

CHAPTER 14

While Ben's call to Attorney Dunn was ringing, another one came in. His Caller ID registered: MACKENZIE. He hit the "Decline" button. His housing car-wreck would have to wait until tonight.

"Dunn," the attorney answered in a hostile tone of voice.

"This is Ben Wallace. I am calling you back as you requested. I spoke with Mr. and Mrs. Westwood about the patent issue you raised."

"And?"

"The recent patent application was filed by Arnold Westwood. It is for an invention that could not even be built today. The Westwoods apologized, but they just forgot to mention it to me in the rush to prepare everything for the sale of their company to your clients. They are honorable people."

"Well, that is just not good enough. How do I know they weren't doing this behind TECH-AI's back to take the money and then put my clients out of business?"

"You have my assurance," Ben replied.

"Not enough," Dunn shot back.

"I'm sorry to hear that."

"Look, Wallace, here's how it is going to play. I'm going to prepare an amendment to the contract to give my clients the exclusive rights to all future inventions and patents attributable to Arnold Westwood for the rest of his life. This is non-negotiable."

"That was never contemplated in the contract," Ben immediately responded, his voice growing more forceful. "The Westwoods felt badly about this oversight and are willing to have this new patent application included in the sale at no additional cost."

"You don't get it, kid," Dunn countered. "It isn't up to the generosity of these two old people. Either my clients get the exclusive lifetime rights to Arnold Westwood's ideas, or we bring suit like I said earlier today."

Ben held his rising temper in check. He knew better than to get into a shouting match with Dunn.

"Mr. Dunn, I don't appreciate your condescending tone, but I will take your proposal back to my clients."

"I'll email the amendment to you in a couple of hours."

"I will present it to my clients for their comments," Ben replied.

"No, Sir. Take it or leave it. Good until 5pm tomorrow, at which point the deal will be off. "

Dunn abruptly hung up.

At that moment, Ben's boss, Neil Martin, unexpectedly walked into his office. He was the younger of the twin brothers, who founded Martin & Martin, born one minute later than his brother. Neil and Ned looked amazing alike, and at the firm, Ned always wore a red tie and Neil always wore a blue tie so that people could easily tell them apart.

Ben joined the firm because of their blue-blood roster of partners who were some of the major stars in the corporate finance and mergers and acquisitions fields, and because he was offered a fast track to partnership.

What he did not realize was that the Martin brothers had come from very modest means, done relatively poorly in law school, had worked out of a storefront next to their parents' tavern on the West side of Chicago doing fender-bender and slip-and-fall cases, and were only able to reach the stratosphere of law firms after they won a $100 million wrongful death lawsuit and collected a $40 million fee.

From that point, Martin & Martin was transformed into a high-pressure performance machine that had been built on enticing famous lawyers to join the firm by offering them huge sign-on bonuses with promises of large annual profit-sharing payouts. The old-world, white-shoe law firm the public saw was really a pressure cooker of competition, egos and shifting loyalties behind the scenes.

Of the two brothers, Neil was the more refined and Ned was just downright greedy, manipulative and competitive. The fact that they both had Ben in their sights about the Westwoods' sale made him feel like he was walking on a high wire above a pit filled with hungry alligators.

"Wallace ..." Neil Martin said in a stern tone.

CHAPTER 15

Neil Martin was standing directly in front of Ben's desk.

"How's the Westwood deal coming?" he asked.

"You know, progress ... a few wrinkles ... but there is communication on the details," Ben answered, carefully choosing his words.

"Wrinkles?"

"From our end, the Westwoods are on track. The buyer's attorney, Charles Dunn, is just throwing his weight around ... in my opinion."

Ben felt himself begin to sweat under his arms.

"Watch out for Dunn, he's a sneaky SOB," Martin cautioned. "He's known for blowing up deals, filing expensive lawsuits and using them to force the price of acquisitions down. Good test for you. We'll be able to see if you are partner material."

"Yes, Sir," Ben replied, trying to put a smile on his face.

"Keep me in the loop. We're counting on this deal closing on time and we're counting on you to make it happen."

Neil Martin's cell phone rang. He walked out of Ben's office as he answered the call.

Ben closed his eyes and took a deep breath. Bullets were coming at him from all sides.

Suddenly, he remembered his father's RV. Where was he going to park it in his neighborhood? And the tux for Gillian's dinner party?

Ben pulled the keyboard of his computer closer and jumped on the internet. Maybe Amazon would bring him salvation.

CHAPTER 16

Ben decided to wait to tell the Westwoods about the proposed amendment to their deal. He wanted to see it first and then he'd have something concrete to explain to them.

His hunt on Amazon for a tuxedo, however, did not go well, but Google came to his rescue, and he wound up on the Macy's website. He had never owned a tuxedo and was amazed at the accompanying parts that need to be purchased, in addition to the jacket and trousers. Once he settled on a tux, he realized he would need a tuxedo shirt, cufflinks (something he also never owned before), shirt studs (because he couldn't find one with buttons), a clip-on bow tie, something called a "cummerbund" and shiny-leather tuxedo shoes. By the time he was finished loading up his online shopping cart, the total made him choke. Gillian's surprise dinner party was going to cost all the available credit left on his reserve credit card. The only good news was that he could have it tomorrow because Macy's used DoorDash for expedited delivery, at an additional cost of course.

Ben shook his head in disbelief, but what choice did he have. He filled out the delivery and credit card information and hit the button to place the order. An email confirmation arrived almost instantly and by tomorrow at this time, he would be the proud owner of his first tuxedo, a fact that he was ambivalent about.

Since it was only mid-afternoon, he had time to kill until he heard from Attorney Dunn. He decided to head home and try to solve the RV parking problem.

His Fulton Market neighborhood was one of the hottest in Chicago. A meat packing and warehouse district dating back to 1850, it had recently been transformed into an emerging, upscale neighborhood with trendy restaurants, art galleries, loft laboratories and expensive condominiums. When Google built two large office buildings in the district and McDonald's moved its Global Headquarters there, the future direction of Fulton Market was clear. There was a buzz in the restaurants and coffee shops as young computer programmers and internet entrepreneurs spoke about new iPhone apps and venture capital vending.

Between the massive amount of construction in progress and the young people moving into the area, parking, however, was a serious problem. Ben knew that finding space on the street for an RV would be out of the question. His best, and only idea, was to stop at a nearby construction site and see his friend Sammy whose company was building a 25-story loft office/condo building.

Sammy was in the construction trailer, on the phone, when Ben arrived.

"You want to park an RV in this neighborhood?" Sammy asked, not hiding his surprise.

"Look, my mom told me that my dad bought some kind of RV and the family was coming up to visit me for Christmas. They were driving it, and my dad wants me to arrange a safe place for him to park it while they are here."

"How long is this thing?"

"I don't know," Ben replied. "I looked up RVs on the internet and they seem to be 25-30 feet long. Can you make that work?"

"Ben, only for you," Sammy said as he reached to answer a phone that was ringing. "I can do 30 feet max. And I mean max. No power or water though. Just a safe space in the staging area for this construction site. OK?"

Ben nodded and shook Sammy's hand. He was relieved that another problem had found a solution and for the moment, he thought he was doing pretty well: air mattresses and bedding were on the way, his tux would be delivered tomorrow and now he had a free parking space for his parents' RV for the entire week.

As he walked to his apartment, Ben believed that his life might actually be coming under control.

CHAPTER 17

No sooner had Ben arrived home when the weather app on his phone beeped an alert. A major winter storm was coming across the Plains and a fierce blizzard was heading directly for Chicago. The snow was expected to arrive tomorrow night, Tuesday, around 9pm.

Ben read it, but it didn't sink in because he was so focused on the Westwood deal. Waiting for Charles Dunn's amendment was wearing on him so much that he didn't even hear the apartment front door open or realize that Mackenzie had walked in.

"You don't answer my calls. You don't return my messages. Am I invisible?" Mackenzie asked, taking Ben by surprise.

"Mackenzie, wow, I wasn't expecting you home so early. Everything alright at the hospital?" Ben tried to buy a few seconds to compose himself.

"Ben, this is not fair. We told you. Did you make the hotel reservations for your parents? And we don't hear back from you."

Mackenzie's face was growing flush. She was really frustrated with him.

"Look, I'm having a very hard day," Ben replied. "My big deal is hanging by a thread. It will either make or break my career. If it breaks, you won't have to worry about me as a roomie. I'll be out of job and broke. I hope you can understand ..."

Mackenzie cut him off. "We all have our problems, Ben.

Would you like to hear about my day in the Emergency Room with a six-year-old girl who was shot in the head and had a stray bullet lodged in her brain? She died in my arms. Would you like to compare days?"

Ben went over to her and put his arms around her to offer some comfort.

"I'm sorry. My problems are minor in comparison. I'll ..."

An incoming text suddenly announced itself on Ben's phone. It was from his secretary with the amendment attached.

"Mackenzie, I'm sorry, but I've got to take this."

Ben went into his bedroom and read the amendment. It was punitive, confiscatory and the ultimate deal-killer. How was he going to break it to the Westwoods? Or his bosses?

CHAPTER 18

Ben's momentary world of silent panic upon reading the Dunn Amendment to the Westwood contract was disrupted by a call from Gillian. He hit "Decline" and put her off for now, even though he knew he would be risking her ire.

His first order of business was to get to the Westwoods and explain the turn of events with their deal.

"Betty," Ben began when she picked up his phone call, "It's Ben Wallace. There has been a development."

"Oh ... "

"I would like to explain things in person. Are you and Arnold available in about an hour?"

"Of course, why don't you come over to our apartment. You know the address, don't you? We're in the Gold Coast."

"I do," Ben replied. "I'll be there."

He pulled up the Uber app on his phone and ordered a car, since parking in the Westwood's neighborhood was impossible. In an ironic way, being chauffeured to his professional funeral seemed like a fitting way to end his brief legal career.

CHAPTER 19

The Wallace RV pulled into the parking lot of the Walmart Superstore near downtown Springfield, Illinois. Anderson Wallace told everyone to sit tight while he made arrangements to park overnight. Inside the store, he asked to see the Manager. About fifteen minutes later, Anderson walked back to the RV.

"Good news," he announced, "We can park right here as long as we want. No problem. Get your things together family."

"That was easy," Molly remarked.

"I made a call last night and was told to stop in and say hello to the store manager. Awfully nice fellow. Was expecting us. Couldn't have been more accommodating."

"Are you surprised?" Molly asked.

"Can I have everyone's attention, please," Anderson said. "We're staying at a nearby Ramada. We have three rooms, plenty for everyone, and the dogs, too. We're going in groups. I'll be driving the SUV we've been trailing, and mom will stay here and be with the last group."

"And tomorrow, we're going to visit your Aunt Katherine, my favorite sister," Molly piped in, "and see her new office. It's right around the capitol. And maybe the tomb of President Lincoln. Won't that be fun! But tonight, we're getting PIZZA!"

"YEA!" everyone joined in.

For the next hour, Anderson shuttled his family to the

hotel and made reservations to take them to the best pizza restaurant in Springfield.

CHAPTER 20

Ben arrived at the Westwoods' apartment building on Astor Street in Chicago's Gold Coast neighborhood. Filled with mansions and row houses from the late-1800s through the Wall Street crash of 1929, and more recent high-rise apartment buildings, the quiet, tree-lined streets offered a suburban-like refuge from the bustle of Chicago's shopping and business districts just blocks away.

The doorman had been alerted to Ben's arrival and ushered him to the elevator. Despite the Westwoods significant wealth, they lived modestly in a two-bedroom apartment on the fourth floor, with a pleasant view of the street. Betty was standing at her front door and greeted him with a welcoming smile.

"This must be really important for you to pay us a personal visit, Ben."

"Betty, I'm afraid it is."

"Come on in and have a seat in the living room."

Arnold was standing by the windows, leafing through a thick book, seemingly oblivious to the world around him other than to say, "Ben ..."

"Coffee, iced tea, maybe a soda?" Betty asked.

"No, thank you," Ben replied as he took a seat on their living room couch. Although the room was neat and tidy, it was clear that the Westwoods were not the kind of people who devoted much attention to furnishings.

Betty sat across from him in her favorite chair.

"Betty ... Arnold," Ben began slowly, "I am sorry, but I have some very difficult news to convey."

Ben took two copies of the amendment from his briefcase and handed one to Betty and one to Arnold.

"I think you both know how hard I have been working for you to make this deal happen the way you want. However, I just received this, about an hour ago, from the buyers' attorney. It is an amendment to the Purchase Agreement that I cannot recommend you accept."

Betty quickly scanned the document. Arnold kept leafing through the book, clearly deferring to his wife.

"What's the bottom line?" Betty asked.

"TECH-AI," Ben replied, "wants a penalty clause of $100 million if any of your patents are invalidated or superseded by new patents and they want all of the future patents you file during the next twenty years to be exclusively owned by them. If you don't agree, they are threatening to sue for huge damages and tie up your company in litigation for years."

Ben was crestfallen for the Westwoods.

"As I said, I cannot recommend that you entertain this amendment. It is, in my opinion, confiscatory and punitive. Of course, the decision is yours."

Betty looked over at Arnold.

"We need a minute in private, please," Betty said as she motioned for Arnold to join her in the kitchen. "We'll be right back."

CHAPTER 21

Back at Ben's apartment, Mackenzie was crying when Siobhan came home from the office.

"Honey, I don't know what to do," Mackenzie blurted out between tears.

Siobhan took her in her arms.

"Whatever it is, it will be alright. I am here now," Siobhan said.

"It's Ben. He keeps avoiding my calls and when I saw him just a little while ago, he was suddenly called away for some emergency at work. I am so upset ..."

"Don't worry, Mackie, I've got this. When Ben comes home, I'll take over. You be the good soul and I'll be the bad cop. I like that role better anyway. It's what I do at work almost every day."

Mackenzie began to calm down.

"Ben is going to have to toe the line," Siobhan continued. "It is our apartment. I'll read him the riot act. His family will have to stay in a hotel. No ifs, ands or buts about it."

"Thanks," Mackenzie said. "I knew you would make it all better."

CHAPTER 22

Betty and Arnold came back into the living room from their kitchen.

"Ben," Betty began, "please excuse my language, but tell those kids of TECH-AI to go screw themselves. We will find another buyer for the company. People who deal fairly. I'm sorry, I know how hard you have been working on our behalf, but there will be other opportunities. And don't worry about their threats of a lawsuit. It comes with the territory."

"I'll let the buyers' attorney know your decision," Ben replied.

"We respect your forthrightness and your honesty. We really appreciate your looking out for us and our interests," Betty added.

Ben collected his briefcase.

"Thanks for coming by and doing this in person," Arnold added.

"Betty ... Arnold, I not only respect your decision, but I also applaud it. You are so much like my parents, and I am honored to be working with you."

Betty showed him to the front door, and with a wry smile said, "Go get 'em!"

In the lobby of the Westwood's building, Ben ordered an Uber and waited by the front door. His mind was racing with thoughts about his call to Attorney Dunn, and about the likely end of his aspirations of becoming a partner at Martin

& Martin.

In the Uber, he wrote himself a text with the key points he would be ready to emphasize to Dunn, depending on how the call went.

As the car turned west on Grand Avenue toward his apartment, his earlier conversation with Mackenzie popped into his head. He had no idea how he was going to solve that problem, but he knew he was about to walk into a storm.

CHAPTER 23

Aunt Katherine showed up at Luigi's Chicago Pizza, reputed to be the best pizza restaurant in Southern Illinois, and was so pleased to see her family all assembled, except for Ben, of course.

She went around the table and gave everyone a big hug and kiss and introduced herself to Nanny Sara.

"What did we order?" Katherine asked. "I hope it was ... PIZZA!"

Billy and Lily cheered.

"Yes, silly, PIZZA!" they shouted together.

Everyone at the table laughed and shouted, "YEA!"

"And how is Ben?" Katherine asked Molly.

"Well, we just don't know. I think that's the main reason we decided to spend Christmas with him. Frankly, I'm worried that being a lawyer is chewing him up. He's such a nice, fair-minded young man."

Molly started to tear up and Anderson reached into his pocket and handed her a small travel pack of tissues.

"Molly," Katherine replied, "I wouldn't worry about him too much. He's young and needs some knocks. Remember when I joined that firm of all men in Chicago? Do you think that was easy? And now look at me, surrounded by all men again. Time for us women to teach men a thing or two."

Anderson listened from across the table but kept his head down and stayed out of the line of fire.

"I'm going to call Ben right now so you can say hello,"

Molly said. "I'll bet he will be very glad to hear from you." Molly dialed Ben's number and listened to it ring.

CHAPTER 24

Before he exited his Uber, Ben called Attorney Dunn's cell phone, but it went instantly to voicemail. He left a message and then tried Dunn's office line. Same result.

When Ben opened the front door to his apartment, it was as he feared. Mackenzie and Siobhan were seated in the living room waiting for him. He felt like a gazelle surrounded by a pride of hungry lionesses. He knew it never ended well for the gazelle.

No sooner had he removed his overcoat than his phone rang. The Caller ID read: MOM.

Ben held up hand to his roommates and shook his head apologetically.

"I'm sorry, I've got to take this," he said and answered the call.

"Mom, I can't talk right now ..."

"It's me, your Aunt Katherine. I thought I would wish you a Merry Christmas!"

Ben took a second to shift mental gears.

"The same to you, Aunt Katherine," he finally replied. "How is your visit going? I hear there are two new puppies on the trip."

"I'm sitting here with the whole family having pizza. I hope to see you soon. I have a hearing in Chicago just after the New Year. Maybe we can have dinner."

"I would love that," Ben responded. "Please forgive me but I am in the middle of something that ... well, that is kind of important."

Ben said goodbye and turned his attention to his room-mates.

"Ladies," he began, "is there a problem?"

CHAPTER 25

Just as Ben turned his full attention to his roommates, his phone rang again. The Caller ID read: CHARLES DUNN.

He excused himself and went into his room.

"Mr. Dunn ..."

"What's your answer, Wallace?"

"With all due respect," Ben replied, "my clients instructed me to decline the amendment you proposed."

"You realize, Wallace, that this means my clients are going to war with yours."

"My clients are aware. They are prepared."

"You understand that I have been instructed to tie up your client's company in court for the next five years or until they capitulate."

Dunn's tone was growing increasingly threatening.

"Look, Mr. Dunn, let me make it clear to you, because of your insistence on the amendment, the deal between TECH-AI and the Westwoods is dead. You and your clients have not been honorable, and my clients will not do business with people like that."

"Are you making a Bar complaint against me, sonny, because if you are, go for it. I will show you how that game is played," Dunn shouted into the phone.

"Mr. Dunn, respectfully," Ben replied softly, resisting the urge to get into the mud with him, "you have been informed how the Westwoods feel, and you will just have to do whatever you have to do."

"Wallace, we're coming for you. See you in court!"

Dunn abruptly hung up.

Ben noticed that his hands were shaking and was glad that no one could see it. He took a few minutes to let the call's impact fade before walking back into the living room "gazelle-kill-zone."

CHAPTER 26

Siobhan took the lead as Ben sat down on the couch. He tried to remain calm on the outside, but knew he was up against a formidable opponent.

Named after a famous Irish actress whose name meant "God's grace," Siobhan Kelly's family emigrated from Dublin to New York City just before she was born. After high school, she went off to Stanford to study finance where she graduated #1 in her class. Thereafter, she moved to Chicago and earned her MBA at the University of Chicago and was quickly hired by a reclusive billionaire to join his private equity firm. Her portfolio was high tech companies and healthcare, and she was known in her field for being a relentless competitor with an unfeeling hot temper that matched the intensity of her short-cropped, flaming red hair.

Siobhan realized that she liked girls over boys by the time she was thirteen. In her junior year in high school, she had a secret love affair with Jenny Greene. To her parents and the outside world, they were just great pals, but it turned into her first sexual relationship during the summer between junior and senior years.

From the earliest days of her sexual discovery, she covered it over by adopting an aggressive attitude. When she realized that she was smarter than almost everyone, she learned how to bully and distract people from finding out she was a lesbian. Sometimes her attitude came off as rough around the edges and she vowed regularly to work on that.

From college on, Siobhan had a long string of love affairs. She had an intellect and a personality that people were drawn to, but when suitors got too close, she pushed them away.

Her love life, however, changed the moment she met Mackenzie.

Their first encounter was at the University of Chicago Hospital when Siobhan was having her appendix removed. Mackenzie was in medical school on her surgery rotation.

It was love at first sight.

Mackenzie McAlister came from Minneapolis and was of Irish-Scottish descent. She was a star athlete in high school, playing basketball and field hockey. A quiet and sometimes shy person, Mackenzie nevertheless had a competitor's heart.

She didn't know that she was gay until her first year at Harvard. A succession of girlfriends, who often became lovers, pushed her to come out to her family at the start of her junior year. Her tall, willowy stature, with flowing amber hair, belied how fragile and vulnerable she could be.

A deep, dark secret that she told no one, however, always haunted her. She had been sexually molested when she was 13 by her uncle, who was a frequent overnight guest at her home. No one else in her family knew and she kept it bottled up inside, even from Siobhan.

After Harvard, where she graduated #2 in her class, Mackenzie went to the University of Chicago Medical School on a full scholarship. She met Siobhan in the University of Chicago Hospital on the day Siobhan had her appendix removed. The chemistry between them was unmistakable and they have been together for over two years.

Siobhan and Mackenzie decided to move in together a year ago and rented a spacious, albeit expensive, loft apartment in the Fulton Market district in Chicago. The location was convenient for Siobhan to be at her office in under fifteen minutes and Mackenzie could jump on the highway and be at the hospital in twenty minutes. They liked the energy of the neighborhood and felt safe and accepted as they dined at the trendy restaurants that lined Fulton Street.

Since both women were very conscious about money, a trait from their respective upbringings, they decided to rent out their second bedroom to help defray the cost of their loft.

Ben was the perfect tenant. He respected their privacy and overlooked their moods. He always talked about growing up with two older sisters and that's how he thought of them.

"There is no way that your entire family can stay in our apartment for a week, much less a single night," Siobhan began. "This is our sanctuary. Both Mackenzie and I have very stressful jobs and we prize the serenity and quiet of this apartment."

"I realize that," Ben replied, waiting for the axe to fall.

"You have been a great roommate," Siobhan continued, "because you understand what it is we need from a home, and you have always been respectful of that. But we just can't see our way clear to turning our sanctuary into a dorm for your family. That's a lot to ask of us."

After the confrontation with Attorney Dunn, Ben was grateful for Siobhan's reasonableness.

"As I have told you, I come from very humble people," Ben began. "My parents are multi-generational apple farmers from Iowa. They are very hard working and really thoughtful. They supported my dream to become a lawyer, even though they were heartbroken that I was not going to work in the family business. They scrimped to pay my law school tuition so that I would not have any student debt and could build a career for myself."

"Ben," Siobhan responded, "we are not doubting any of that. I am sure your parents are lovely, caring people. It's just that we have to look out for ourselves. We can't afford to do our jobs if we are exhausted and stressed-out. Why don't they stay at a hotel? Isn't that the solution staring you in the face?"

"I don't think they could afford that," Ben replied, "moreover, that's just not how our family thinks. They would be deeply offended. We stick together and help each other out. Staying here would mean a lot to them. And to me. I don't want to embarrass them."

Ben's mind was beginning to race. He needed to find another solution, and fast.

"Well," Mackenzie said, "I guess we are at an impasse. Siobhan, what are we going to do?"

"Wait!" Ben exclaimed, as an idea popped into his head. "How about this. I am going to get a nice Christmas bonus from my law firm in the next two weeks. What if I buy you a trip to Puerta Vallarta and pay all the expenses for seven nights? You will both have the best time. I was there a few years ago on holiday. The weather and the ocean were perfect, the hotel was excellent and the food outstanding. You will be pampered and cared for. It will be the getaway you have been talking about taking for years, but never did. Will that work? Can you cut me some slack?"

Ben realized what he was saying as the words came out of his mouth. Paying down his credit cards was just going to have to wait.

"You would do that for us?" Mackenzie asked.

"I know you need your space," Ben continued. "I love rooming with you both and I really would appreciate not having to move out. Of course, it's your apartment and up to you."

Ben hoped he had been persuasive.

"What will your parents think about us?" Siobhan asked. "Are they ready to stay in the same apartment with a lesbian couple? If there is going to be friction ..."

"Not a problem," Ben replied, without thinking it through too much. "They are conservative, but very tolerant people. Hell, they were willing to allow me to become a lawyer and I will refrain from telling you their opinion of lawyers."

Siobhan looked at Mackenzie, who nodded her approval.

"Alright, here's the deal," Siobhan said, "just keep your family out of our bedroom and especially out of our bathroom. They can use your bathroom and the powder room. That's non-negotiable. And they have to be quiet at night so we can get our sleep."

"Sure ... sure," Ben agreed. "Sounds perfectly fine to me."

As a feeling of peace started to fill the room, Ben suddenly remembered that he had to call the Westwoods and tell them about his call with Attorney Dunn.

CHAPTER 27

Betty Westwood answered Ben's call.

"Hi, Ben!"

"Betty, I spoke with TECH-AI's attorney and told him that you were not interested in accepting the proposed amendment to the contract," Ben said.

"And how did he take it?"

"Not well. He said he had been instructed to tie up your company with lawsuits for the next five years."

"You know," Betty replied, "it works both ways."

"I'm afraid if Dunn carries out his threat, this litigation is going to be expensive."

"Never give in to bullies, Ben. If you do, they never stop. Arnold and I understand the circumstances and we are prepared to spend whatever it takes. In the end, we know we did nothing wrong."

"What if they change their minds about the amendment and want to go forward? What do you want to do?" Ben asked.

"We will honor the contract to the letter, of course. Frankly, all this emotional pushing and shoving before a deal closes isn't foreign to us. People try to throw their weight around and sometimes you just have to look passed it. The essence of the deal is sound. Their behavior is just juvenile. Now, you just go about your business and let's see what happens. Don't worry about it. We certainly are not."

Ben was relived as he ended the call. He was amazed at

Betty's calm demeanor and steady hand. He was learning a lot from them.

His momentary reflection, however, hit a speed bump when his phone rang. The Caller ID read: GILLIAN.

CHAPTER 28

"Gillian!" Ben said as he answered her call.

Ben met Gillian on a blind date six months ago. He was immediately attracted to her statuesque figure and her penetrating blue eyes that were framed by her long, auburn hair. Every word that came out of her mouth exuded poise and confidence. She was so unlike the girls he had grown up with in Iowa.

Of course, what Ben did not understand was that Gillian's persona was as manufactured as processed American cheese. She concealed her rural, middle class, Pennsylvania background, her in-State college because that's all her parents could afford and she made people think of her as an Ivy League "influencer" who, at 24, was on her way to fame and fortune. Verbal, charming, when she saw the need to be, she was a social shark and social climber with no filter to modulate her ambitions.

All Ben saw, however, was an energetic, attractive young woman, popular with men and women alike, and someone that people wanted to know and to be with. What Ben couldn't see was her tough, disciplined, egocentric, narcissistic and unforgiving agenda to make her way, at all costs, into the upper echelons of society.

She had had only one serious boyfriend before Ben, and she dumped him when she realized that he would not be a good vehicle for her ambitions. She thought Ben might be the ticket because of his boy-next-door good looks and his position at a very prestigious Chicago law firm. Together they made a striking couple, and she knew she could use that to her advantage. As long as he didn't talk about his growing up on a farm, she felt he enhanced her, but did not overshadow her.

"Ben, I'm so excited about this party at the Art Institute. There are going to be so many important people that we need to meet. And my dress is going to look like I just stepped off the cover of *Vogue*. People are really going to notice. I want them to think of us as the young couple everyone wants to be!"

Ben just listened. This was way beyond his pay grade.

"And I bought these shoes ... everyone will be talking about them. The five-inch heals make my legs looks like I'm on a fashion runway. I know I'm spending a lot of money, but this is really going to be worth it."

"... great," Ben said.

"You've got your tux, right? And it looks fabulous, right?"

"Yes, Gillian, it's coming ..."

"And it looks fabulous, right?"

"Fabulous," Ben replied even though he had no idea how it was going to look. Based on his body-type, clothes just naturally fit him perfectly. In another life, he could have been a model.

His mind started to drift while Gillian continued to talk about the party. A text pulled him back to the here and now. It was from Amazon. His order for air mattresses and bedding was going to be delayed until the day after his parents arrived. The reason given was a massive winter storm about to engulf Chicago.

"Gillian," Ben said, beginning to panic, "I've got to go.

There's an emergency. We can talk tomorrow. Bye."

Ben looked at the weather app on his phone. Since he arrived home, the weather had turned ugly and was going to get much, much worse. Something like a foot of snow in the coming days was predicted.

The only thing Ben could think about was that he had to find air mattresses and right away. He went to his computer and started to search. Target and Walmart came up. There was a large Target not too far from his apartment.

CHAPTER 29

Ben didn't realize that he had fallen asleep at his desk before he finished his order for air mattresses. It was one of his roommates slamming their bedroom door that jolted him awake.

"I can't take it," Mackenzie shouted as she stormed into Ben's room. "Every time I try to be nice to her, she scolds me about something else."

Mackenzie fell onto Ben's bed, curled up in a fetal position and started to cry uncontrollably.

Ben wasn't expecting this. He went over to comfort her.

"Mac, it can't be that bad," he said as he sat down next to her and gently stroked her head.

"Yes, it is!"

"People have differences of opinion. Happens all the time. To everyone."

"She's mean. I hate her," Mackenzie said as she struggled to catch her breath between sobs.

"Look, honey, you just need to explain how you feel to her. She's a very bright woman. She can figure it out. She loves you," Ben said in a soothing tone.

"Do you think so?" Mackenzie asked, looking up at him.

"Of course I do. Look, you can stay here tonight, if that makes you feel better. You can sleep on my bed, and I'll sleep at my desk. No problem ..."

"Ben, you're a prince. Thank you."

"I've got something I have to do. You just relax and get

some sleep."

He covered her with his comforter and returned to his desk.

Ten minutes later, his air mattress problem had a solution. Target had plenty of them, including all the sheets and pillows he needed. He made a pickup order for 8am and cancelled his Amazon order.

For the first time that day he breathed a sigh of relief. He leaned back in his chair, closed his eyes, and promptly fell asleep.

It was the text from Charles Dunn at 4am that startled him back to consciousness.

CHAPTER 30

Attorney Dunn's text read: "My clients can live without the amendment. Closing is still on for 1pm on Christmas Eve."

Ben wasn't going to text Dunn back until he spoke to the Westwoods, and he wasn't going to call them at four in the morning. Dunn would have to wait.

He looked over a Mackenzie. For such an emotionally fragile person, she looked rather peaceful and composed as she slept.

"What the hell!" Siobhan shouted as she burst into Ben's room. "Your f-ing text woke me up. Can't you learn to silence your phone at night? Is there something wrong with you?"

"Nice to see you, too," Ben replied. "Busy night here."

Mackenzie started to wake up and seemed confused as to where she was.

"Mackie, I'm sorry," Siobhan said apologetically, as she sat on the edge of Ben's bed. "I've been under so much stress. I didn't mean to take it out on you."

A smile appeared on Mackenzie's face and Siobhan leaned over and kissed her on the forehead.

"Come back to bed," Siobhan said. "We can work this out in the morning. It's nothing to worry about. I love you."

Half asleep, Mackenzie nodded and rolled out of Ben's bed.

Hand-in-hand the two women left Ben's room.

Now, Ben thought, *the universe is finally getting itself together.* What he didn't realize was how hard it had begun to snow.

CHAPTER 31

Ben overslept. He had set his phone alarm for 7am but neglected to flip the switch to green. It was 8:30am when he opened his eyes and realized how late he was. Showering was out. He only had time to shave, brush his teeth and climb into yesterday's suit.

Ten minutes later, he called the Westwoods from his car.

"Betty, I have good news," Ben began. "I received a text in the middle of the night from the buyers' attorney. They have abandoned their demand for the amendment and are planning to show up at the closing."

"Well," Betty replied, "that will be just fine. Thank you, Ben."

His next call was to his secretary, Jessie, to let her know he would be coming in late today.

As the snow kept falling at about an inch per hour, Ben headed to the Target on Division Street just west of the Gold Coast. He liked that store because it had plenty of covered parking.

He was a man on a mission. When the store couldn't locate his online pickup order, he found a store employee to help him round up one full-sized air mattress and five singles, plus sheets, pillows, pillowcases and blankets. At the checkout station, when the total came to over $1,200, he was taken aback.

"One second," he told the clerk as he searched for his debit card. Since his credit cards were nearing their limits, his alternative was to use the last bit of cash he had in his account. He would just have to make do until his father reimbursed him in a few days. At least his gas tank was full.

A store employee helped him stuff everything into his Toyota Corolla, and as he drove out of the store's garage, he saw that the snowfall had picked up its pace. His office would have to wait a bit longer. He headed back to his apartment to drop off his purchases.

No sooner had he brought the last of the bedding supplies into his living room than Jessie called with some bad news. Arnold Westwood was just taken by ambulance to Northwestern Memorial Hospital's emergency room.

CHAPTER 32

When the Wallace family arrived at the address of Aunt Katherine's office, they were quite surprised. Walking into the Illinois Supreme Court building was awe-inspiring.

"Can you direct us to Katherine Grant's office?" Molly asked the uniformed guard at the front desk.

"You'll have to wait here. I need to see photo IDs for each of the adults to run through security," he responded in a very formal tone.

Molly thought it was a lot of trouble just to visit a court employee.

With that, Katherine Grant appeared on the other side of the security barrier.

"Cecil, it's alright. They are my family."

"Yes, Madame Chief Justice," he replied and buzzed them through.

Anderson and Molly's surprise was palpable.

"I thought you might be arriving now," Katherine said, "come with me."

She led the group down a long hall.

"You never ..." Molly said.

"You never asked," Katherine replied. "Let me give you a brief tour. It's quite a building with lots of history."

After the tour, she led everyone to the Chief Justice's cavernous office.

Katherine Grant, Molly's older sister, never married. After completing her law degree at Harvard on a full scholarship and a clerkship for the Chief Justice of the Federal Appellate Court in Washington, D.C., one of Chicago's largest and most prestigious law firm made her an offer she couldn't refuse. She quickly developed a thriving appellate court practice and a national reputation.

When one of the Illinois Supreme Court Justices announced her retirement, the other members of the Supreme Court elected Aunt Katherine to the open seat, and two years later, they unanimously chose her to be the Chief Justice.

She moved to Springfield from Chicago when she first went on the Supreme Court, and she had always hoped that her sister and family would find the time to visit one day. When Ben passed the Illinois Bar and joined Martin & Martin, she sent him a special fountain pen to commemorate his achievement and always asked her sister for a status report on his progress.

"I guess you have done alright for yourself, Sis," Molly remarked as she and her grandchildren took seats on the chairs in front of a massive desk.

"Am I more interesting to you now, Anderson?" Katherine asked with a twinkle in her eye.

"I suppose ... but we need to be on our way. I heard there's a big storm up north of here and I don't want us to get stuck."

"Anderson," Molly interrupted. "You're a stick in the mud."

"Molly ..." he responded.

"Alright," she replied, "it's probably best that we leave Aunt Katherine to her very important work. We've got to get packed and take care of the dogs. We're leaving early tomorrow morning and driving straight into a blizzard!"

CHAPTER 33

Just as Ben was about to call Betty's cell, a call from Charles Dunn interrupted him.

"Wallace, we need the latest financials for the past 60 days, right up until today, and we need them by tomorrow noon. Certified by the Westwoods' accountants as true and correct. Got that ... certified!"

"Mr. Dunn, I just found out a few minutes ago that Arnold Westwood was taken to the hospital by ambulance. I was about to call for more information when you called. We might have to push the closing back a few days or a week," Ben replied.

"Absolutely not!" Dunn shouted. "We close on Friday or not at all."

"Certainly, you can understand that health emergencies should be taken into account."

"Not in my world. The deal closing is set in stone, unless, of course, the Westwoods are trying to pull a financial fast one that gets covered up by the holidays."

"I can assure you," Ben replied, his tone becoming firm, "there is nothing going on under the table. I just thought you would be willing to show some humanity."

"Let me be perfectly clear, young man, NOT IN MY WORLD."

Ben had done everything he could not to get into a spitting contest with Dunn, but Dunn had finally pushed him too far.

"And let me be perfectly clear, Mr. Dunn, my clients have done and will continue to do the right thing. Your clients have been demanding and unreasonable. If you are looking to kill this deal, then take your best shot. My clients are not afraid of your tactics and, frankly, your clients will feel the pain if this goes to court. For now, the closing is on as scheduled. If it needs to be postponed for a medical reason that you don't accept, then we will fight it out in court. I'll see what I can do about the financials. Have a nice day."

Ben disconnected the call and for the first time felt that he had gained some ground.

His next call was to Betty Westwood. It went to voicemail.

Ben decided to head to the hospital to see if there was anything he could do for the Westwoods since they had no children or relatives to lean on. He thought his being there might be of some comfort. Normally, it would have taken him fifteen minutes to get to Northwestern Memorial Hospital from his apartment. Today, however, the snowstorm had a vote.

CHAPTER 34

An hour later Ben finally pulled into the hospital's parking garage. The snow was really coming down and tying up traffic.

He went to the information desk and got a Visitor tag to Arnold Westwood's room.

To his surprise, he found Arnold sitting in a reclining chair with Betty by his side.

"Is everything alright?" Ben asked. "I was really worried when I got the news."

"Of course, dear," Betty replied. "Arnold was having some irregular heart issues and his doctor wanted him to be in the hospital for tests. We'll probably be home tonight. This happens. There is really nothing to worry about."

"Well, I was," Ben said. "And your buyers are still at it. Now they are demanding your latest financials through today – certified by your accountants. They want the numbers by noon tomorrow."

"No problem, Ben. We have nothing to hide."

Betty took her cell phone from her purse, called their accounting firm and told the partner in charge to give Ben whatever he needed right away. Then she handed the phone to Ben so he could explain in more detail.

"Now, Ben," Betty said after he finished up on the call, "thank you for coming to check on us. We're going to be fine. You just carry on."

When Ben left the hospital, he felt much better. That lasted only until he saw how the blizzard had progressed. Going into his office was out of the question. He would have to review the closing documents at home tonight because as soon as his family arrived, it was going to chaos.

He called his secretary and found out that his office had closed for the day because of the weather. Then he saw a text from Macy's. They could deliver his tuxedo jacket and pants and his cufflinks, but the shirt, bow tie, cummerbund and shoes would be delayed for three days because of the storm. Did he still want DoorDash to bring him the partial order today?

Gillian's party was on Thursday night – in two days. He felt his heart rate starting to climb as he imagined her response. He decided to break the news to her when he got home.

CHAPTER 35

No matter how far from his ear Ben held the phone, he could still hear Gillian screaming at him. She was furious at his incompetence at doing something as simple as buying a tuxedo. She actually couldn't believe that he didn't own at least one.

"Don't you realize how important this party is to me?" she carried on. "How could you do this to me? Don't you care about my feelings? About my standing in the community? Without a tux, Ben, I have to cancel. I can't go alone, and it is too late to replace you. This was my big chance to get us into society. Do you know how hard I worked to get this invitation?"

Ben sat down on the floor and leaned against his bookcase in his room.

"Ben, are you listening to me?"

"Yes, Gillian, I'm here."

"What do you have to say for yourself? You couldn't even buy or, God forbid, rent a tux? What's wrong with you?"

She wasn't letting up on the whipping.

"You realize that my life in Chicago could be over before it even starts. I don't know how I will bear the embarrassment of cancelling. What do I say, my date was too much of a hick from Iowa to own a tux and couldn't figure out how to find one?"

Ben finally had had enough.

"Gillian, I'm sorry. It was beyond my control with the weather. If you can't accept that ..."

She cut him off in mid-sentence.

"Maybe you're not the right man for me. You're really going to have to step up your game if you want to be with me."

"Look, I have to work. We can continue this conversation later."

He hung up and held his head in his hands.

Siobhan gently knocked on the door to his room and walked in.

"Girl troubles?"

"How could you tell?"

"Lucky guess. Oh, by the way, you've got a scene from *The Godfather* going on in our living room. It looks like your family is going to 'the mattresses.' You know how I hate clutter."

"Just think Puerta Vallarta and overlook the three-ring circus about to descend. You don't have a spare tux in your closet, do you?"

"Ha, ha! Good luck getting anything delivered in this weather. I don't even know how your family will be able to make it with all the snow."

CHAPTER 36

Ben pulled himself together, shook off the emotional scars that Gillian had inflicting and decided that a slice of pizza would give him some necessary comfort. He found an old box of bake-it-yourself pizza in the freezer and read the instructions. The less preferred method, or so the box read, was to cook the pizza in the microwave. It would be faster by half an hour, but not as "delicious." He was hungry. Ben opted for the microwave version.

While he waited for the pizza to cook, Ben texted his secretary that he would be working from home tomorrow because of the storm and would review the closing documents tonight. He needed her to standby for edits.

No matter how hard he tried, however, he couldn't get the call with Gillian out of his mind. When he got back to his desk, he decided to research where he might be able to rent a tuxedo on an emergency basis. He quickly concluded that because on the weather, a tux was not in his future.

Ben spent the remainder of the night reviewing the 200 pages of closing documents and sending emails to his secretary with slight modifications. She would have to fix everything, highlight the changes tomorrow and email the documents to Attorney Dunn. Ben hoped there would be enough time for he and Dunn to iron out the last-minute details.

CHAPTER 37

It was four in the morning by the time Ben finished reviewing the documents. His alarm at 7am came way too soon.

He shaved and showered in record time, took one more look at his edits of the deal documents and emailed them to Jessie to incorporate and finalize. Once she was done, he would double-check her work and email them to Attorney Dunn.

The smell of fresh coffee lured him into the kitchen. Mackenzie had a knack for brewing the best.

A few sips to wake up, a deep breath of anticipation and then Ben placed *the* call to Gillian.

"I am truly sorry," he began, "but I have to plead 'Act of God' as the reason I couldn't get a tux. It wasn't for lack of trying, but the snowstorm interceded."

"Ben ... I can't tell you how much you have disappointed me. I thought I could count on you. That you would be there as my knight in shining armor. And you just let me down. I am not sure that I can get over this."

"Maybe the event will be cancelled because of the weather," he suggested, in a last-ditch, *Hail Mary* kind of way.

"You'd better pray you're right," Gillian shot back, with an ominous tone in her voice.

After she disconnected the call, Ben noticed that he was beginning to have second thoughts about their relationship.

Since he had about an hour before Jessie would have the revised documents back to him, he decided to organize the bedding he had purchased at Target and looked for the instructions on how the air mattresses worked.

CHAPTER 38

Anderson Wallace got everyone going early on Wednesday morning because of the snowstorm. By 9:30am, the Wallace family was on the road again.

According to Molly's directions app on her phone, the drive from Springfield, Illinois to Chicago was about 200 miles and would take three hours. With the snow, however, the app was predicting that it would take six, at best.

For the first couple of hours, Sara kept Billy and Lily occupied by playing board games and reading stories out loud. Then, she got everyone looking for license plates from different states, shouting out their discoveries as the RV rolled down the highway. That was followed by a singalong that started with *The Wheels on the Bus*, followed by *Old MacDonald*, *Mary Had a Little Lamb* and *The Farmer in the Dell*.

When Sara sensed that the adults had had enough, she put episodes of *Sponge Bob* on the RV's giant flatscreen and gave the kids wireless earbuds so only they could hear the program.

"I'm worried about Ben," Molly confided softly to her husband as she slid into the shotgun seat. "I think he is under a great deal of pressure at the law firm, and I wonder if he is working with the right kind of people."

"I guess we'll have to see for ourselves, won't we?" Anderson replied.

CHAPTER 39

The text message from Ben's mother read:

"Honey, please go to the grocery store and get something for us to eat tonight and tomorrow in case we get snowed in. Nothing too much that needs to be cooked. Cold cuts, salads, lots of fresh fruit, things for breakfast for the kids ... and some snacks for everyone. Maybe some fresh breads. Easy on the sweets, of course. You know what we like."

Ben felt like his head was ready to explode as he read her message. He knew she was right, but it was just one more thing for him to do. This Christmas hometown reunion was going from a bad idea to a living nightmare, and it hadn't even started yet.

Ben went to his laptop, pulled up Amazon's Whole Foods website and ordered what he hoped would be enough to last four or five days. Since Macy's couldn't fulfill his tux order on time, the available credit on his credit card still had enough room. To his surprise, despite the storm, Amazon would have his order delivered around noon.

"Thank you, Jeff Bezos," he mumbled under his breath.

His feeling of accomplishment, however, was short-lived. His phone rang and the Caller ID read: CHARLES DUNN.

CHAPTER 40

"Look, Wallace," Dunn began, "TECH-AI wants to change the deal."

Ben was no longer taken aback by Dunn's antics.

"Mr. Dunn, with all due respect," he replied, "I am just waiting on the final paperwork from my secretary. I was planning on emailing it to you for your last look. I made some very minor housekeeping edits, and they will be highlighted for you to see. This deal is ..."

Dunn cut him off.

"You don't get it, do you, Wallace. My clients are in the drivers' seat. They want to buy this company for $100 million in cash and $150 million in stock, instead of $250 million in cash. Same number, just a slight variation in how it is tendered. Shouldn't be a problem. Certainly isn't from our end."

"Mr. Dunn, that is not the deal that was agreed to."

"Price is the same. I don't see the difference. My clients thought about it. They want the Westwoods to have some skin in the game. A significant stock position keeps them in. Makes sense to us. Do you have a problem?"

"I do," Ben replied. "I'll take your proposal to my clients, but I will not recommend it. A deal is a deal. I don't think you understand that concept."

Ben abruptly disconnected the call. Dunn had finally pushed him too far.

CHAPTER 41

To Ben's surprise, Siobhan was still hanging around the apartment.

"No work today?" he asked.

"Snow day for my office," she replied. "This is the slow time of the year. Most deals wrapped up weeks ago. Yours is the only one that I know of still in play."

"Nothing like carrying water uphill," Ben said, "and into the wind. By the way, I ordered an entire Whole Foods store for my family's visit. They will be delivering in under an hour. Would you mind receiving it for me if I am on a call, and putting the cold things in the fridge?"

Ben gave her his most sympathetic look and hoped.

"You continue to pop into my personal life in unexpected ways," she responded. "What the hell, since it's Christmas, why not ... as long as I can watch you crash and burn over that tuxedo thing. Hilarious."

"I know, it's a dumpster fire."

"When's the next Ben and Gillian installment? It's becoming my guilty pleasure."

"Your cruel streak is showing," he said, knowing she would take it as a compliment.

With that settled, Ben started to call Betty Westwood with an update.

Before he finished entering her number, his phone rang. The Caller ID read: MOM.

CHAPTER 42

"Ben, it's Mom!"

"Hi, Mom, how the trip going?"

"Your father is a marvelous driver, and his new RV is a dream on the road in spite of the snow."

"Just drive safely, please," Ben said.

"We're making great time. Your father estimates that we will be at your apartment in about an hour. Much faster than the the app on my phone said."

"An hour, great, that's fast. I'll be on the lookout."

"And everyone's going to be hungry, so I hope your prepared!"

"I bought out an entire grocery store," Ben responded. "At least from the bill, it seemed like it. It's due to arrive about the time you do."

"Love you, Ben."

"Love you too, Mom."

When his mother hung up, Ben finished dialing Betty Westwood.

CHAPTER 43

On hearing Ben's news Betty Westwood didn't even ask her husband about the changes that the TECH-AI kids were demanding.

"Ben, dear, when you meet people like that, you just have to keep slapping them down. Please tell the attorney that, if they don't want to buy our company, then they can just walk away. We will release them from the deal without enforcing the penalty clause. Life is too short for this kind of nonsense," Betty said.

"Got it," Ben replied. "I completely understand. Very generous of you to waive the penalty clause though."

"We always look ahead, Ben, and going to court to punish these kids would take up too much of our time and everyone would be consumed by negative energy. That's just not how we want to live our lives. I think you can understand that."

Ben was learning so much from her.

"Got it," Ben replied. "I'll let their attorney know."

His next call was to Charles Dunn.

"Mr. Dunn," Ben began the call. "I spoke with Mrs. Westwood. I told her about our last conversation and about your clients' attempt to rewrite the deal."

"What's your point, Wallace. Stop wasting my time."

"As I was trying to say, my clients are prepared to close this deal as negotiated and agreed to. That's it. And, they have graciously offered to waive the penalty for breach against your clients if your people want to walk away. It's alright with the Westwoods. If your clients want to do the deal as agreed, that's alright, too. It's up to your people."

"Look, Wallace, you don't get it. Either the Westwoods agree, or we'll be in Federal court by Friday tying up their company for five years. That's how this transaction is going to play out. I know you are an inexperienced, young attorney. Have you really explained the consequences of not closing this deal to them? Do you even understand what I am saying? This is not an idle threat."

Ben resented Dunn's attitude, but he knew Dunn was trying to bait him and he wasn't going to bite.

"With all due respect, Mr. Dunn, it is you who doesn't understand. The closing is set for 1pm this coming Friday. We set this time to accommodate your clients. A Christmas Eve closing is certainly not usual. Either your clients show up with a cashier's check to close this deal or they don't. My clients don't care whether they do, or they don't. At this point, the Westwoods are done with last minute demands and so am I. I'll send you over the revised documents later this morning. And don't try to use my edits as a pretext. If you don't like them, then we'll go with the original version drafted by your office. I can live with that version, if necessary. My office ... 17th Floor Conference Room ... 1pm ... this Friday. See you then, or not at all. Your choice."

Ben abruptly hung up and realized that his heart was pounding a mile a minute. It was the first time he had ever pushed an opposing counsel's bluff to the wall.

Two minutes later, Ned Martin called him from the law firm.

CHAPTER 44

The lobby buzzer announced the delivery from Whole Foods. The driver left fifteen very full bags in the front vestibule and texted a photo of them to Ben.

When Siobhan saw the distress on Ben's face from the call he was on, she went downstairs to retrieve the bags as promised, although she wasn't expecting so many bags and so many trips down to the lobby and back up to the third floor.

"Sir," Ben said, "I'm doing the best I can. This guy Dunn is an ass. He keeps trying to derail the deal."

"Ben," Ned Martin replied, "just don't blow it. You need to find a way. The fees are already budgeted in the firm's yearend numbers and your bonus is riding on it. Think of it as good for us and good for you."

"I'll do my best," Ben responded, feeling the full weight of his future hanging in the balance.

When the call ended, Ben just leaned against the nearest wall for support.

"Little help here," Siobhan said as she lugged the final bags into the apartment.

"I am so sorry you had to do this alone, but I really appreciate it."

"How much do your people eat?"

"I owe you," Ben replied.

"Really? You've been running a tab with me, and it just got

much, much longer."

"You'll like my family. In fact, they'll be here in under an hour. I can manage the groceries from here. Help yourself to whatever you want. There's plenty ..."

With that they both broke out in laughter. Ben's comment was an understatement.

As they put the groceries away, Ben steeled himself in anticipation of the chaos from Iowa about to descend on his life.

CHAPTER 45

Ben's phone rang. The Caller ID read: MOM.

"We're in front of your apartment building!" Molly announced. "Your father has us double-parked right at the corner of Aberdeen and Hubbard."

"I'll be right down," Ben said as he grabbed his parka and rushed down the hallway stairs.

"HI, BEN!" Molly greeted him with a big hug. "I'm so glad to see you!"

"Hi, Mom."

Ben gave her a big kiss.

"But what the hell ..." he said as he surveyed the vehicle his family had arrived in.

Anderson Wallace came down the front steps of the RV to greet his son.

"Dad, what the hell. This isn't an RV. This is ... I don't know what to call it, but its huge!"

"Nice to see you, too, son."

"I thought you were in a normal RV. I made arrangements to park a 30-foot vehicle at my friend's construction site across the street. This thing must be 45-feet long and what's that ... a trailer with a Tesla SUV? This whole thing must be 65-feet."

"Observant as ever," Anderson remarked.

"Look, Dad, you can't park this thing in this neighborhood. There are no places. I'm not sure what we're going to do."

With that his sister Caitlin exited the RV, gave Ben a hug and a punch on the shoulder. She was followed by his sister Holly who shouted, "BENNY!" and gave him a bear hug.

She was followed by her husband, Todd, and their kids, Billy and Lily.

"Todd," Ben said as they shook hands, "and it's BILLY-LILY!" he teased as if they were one person.

Last to exit was Sara Holcolm, his high school sweetheart. He gave her a polite hug and a smile, but was privately struck by how much more beautiful she was than he remembered.

"I see that you have survived the Wallace circus ... so far," Ben remarked.

"I think they are all great," Sara replied.

Surrounded by his entire family, fresh from the farm, standing in the falling snow, Ben was overwhelmed by the reality of it. So many people, so excited to be at his home. How were they all going to fit in his apartment?

"Come on everybody, let's get out of the cold," Ben said. "Todd, give me a hand with the luggage and Dad, please just hang out by the Brontosaurus. Once the girls are settled and the bags are upstairs, I'll be back down to work out where you are going to park this thing."

CHAPTER 46

"Everyone," Ben shouted above the din in his apartment. "This is Siobhan, one of my roommates." He pointed in her direction.

"Siobhan, this is my family, my mom, Molly, my two sisters, Caitlin and Holly. Holly's husband, Todd. Their two kids, Billy and Lily, and their temporary nanny, Sara. They are fresh off of our family apple farm in Wallaceton, Iowa. It is a town of 900 very proud people, located just south of Davenport. And now they are here in the big city ... I can't believe it ... so everyone, please take off your coats and make yourselves comfortable while I go downstairs and help dad with his dinosaur."

Anderson Wallace had stepped back inside his RV while Ben and Todd took care of the luggage. He was on his cell phone when Ben knocked on the door.

"Dad ..." Ben started to say but was abruptly interrupted by his father holding up his hand, motioning him to stop talking until he finished his call.

"OK, great. Thanks," Anderson said and hung up.

"Dad, I'll find a place for you to park. It might take me a little while, but I'm sure there's a place somewhere."

"Son, no need. See that Tesla parking lot at the end of this block, just across the street? They said I could park there for as long as I wanted."

Ben was stunned. "How?"

"Just had to make a call. Take a seat and we'll get her in place. I'll leave the car there, too. Won't be needing it tonight, will we?"

Anderson Wallace drove his 45-foot Prevost "RV" followed by the 20-foot car trailer holding the Tesla SUV across Grand Avenue and into the parking lot that Tesla used to stage the arrival of newly built cars destined for Chicago customers.

A man came out of the garage, directed him to a safe corner of the lot and reached up to shake his hand.

"Mr. Wallace, welcome!" the Tesla employee said. "It is a pleasure to meet you. Anything we can do, just let me know – day or night. Here's my business card. I put my cell phone number on the back. Really, anything ..."

"Nice of you fellas to give me a hand. Saving my son a lot of grief. He was worried where we could park our little caravan."

"Happy to help, Sir."

After securing the RV, Ben and his father started to walk back to Ben's apartment. The snow had slowed down a bit. Ben was struck by how quiet everything seemed under the thick blanket of fresh snow.

"How dad?" Ben asked.

"I just had to call a guy."

"What guy? Who do you know in Chicago who could pull this off? And one more question, you know, the elephant in the room kind of question, did you mortgage the family farm to buy this 'vehicle.' I mean, I've seen photos of the inside of rockstar buses, and yours is over the top."

"Son," Anderson replied in a matter-of-fact way, "first, it's not your farm, it's my farm. And second, it's none of your damn business. Now tell me about this law firm you work at and this big deal you are trying to close. Nothing confidential, of course."

Ben was surprised by his father's interest but was excited to give him the 30,000-foot view of the Westwoods, their unique company and the difficult buyers. He purposely glossed over how things were going for him at the law firm.

CHAPTER 47

Walking into the apartment only reinforced reality for Ben
that the Wallace family circus had truly come to town. People
were everywhere, talking, sorting out the luggage, moving
the air mattresses around, looking for something to eat and
Billy and Lily were running around opening every closet
door. As large and as roomy as the two-bedroom loft was,
with its high wooden-beamed ceilings and its exposed indus-
trial air conditioning and heating ducts, Ben could see that
this was a lot of people.

"Welcome!" Ben shouted. "I'm glad you are all here, but I've
got to lay down some rules if we're all going to survive this
week."

He nervously glanced in Siobhan's direction, but she didn't
even notice. She was deep in conversation with Ben's sister,
Caitlin.

"OK," he went on, "here are the rules of the road. Mom
and dad can have my room. Everyone else will be bunking on
air mattresses here in the living room. Everyone can use my
bathroom and the powder room. Siobhan and Mackenzie's
room and bathroom are off limits. There's plenty of food
in the fridge, but please, please rinse your dishes and put
them in the dishwasher. The coffee maker is for everyone.
It makes individual cups of whatever you want or whatever
mixture you invent. The TV remote is on the shelf. Please
don't lose it. It's the only one we have. The Wi-Fi password

is written on the chalk board. There are extra towels in the hall closet and the washer and dryer are down the back hall. If you have any questions, you know where I live."

To Ben's surprise, Siobhan piped in.

"Caitlin is going to stay in our room, so that will be one less in the living room and in the bathroom and powder."

With that, Siobhan led Caitlin into her room and shut the door.

Ben took a moment to let it sink in before continuing.

"Look, everyone, I've got to make a business call. So, carry on ..." he said and went downstairs into the vestibule to call the Westwoods to let them know about his last conversation with Attorney Dunn.

CHAPTER 48

"Ben," Betty Westwood replied, after he had summarized his latest skirmish with Attorney Dunn, "you are doing just fine. We will be at your office on Friday, and we will be ready to close the deal. You did the right thing, and we appreciate it."

When the call ended, Ben was pleased with himself. That feeling, however, only lasted until his phone rang again. It was Gillian.

"Ben, the dinner at the Art Institute has been postponed because of the weather. It will be rescheduled for after the holidays. You dodged that bullet, buddy," she said. "So, what are your plans about me meeting your parents. Why don't you come pick me up. I can be ready in an hour. How dressed should I be? What are we going to do tonight?"

Ben looked outside and saw that the snow had started to come down faster.

"Not a good idea, Gilly," he replied. "Have you looked out your window? How about I arrange for you to meet them sometime tomorrow."

"Ben, you know I live on the 25th floor. I can't see what's going on at street level. If you are putting me off, tell me now. Otherwise, I need to know exactly what I am doing and when so that I can get it on my calendar. Why don't you call me back in an hour when you figure this out. You're going to have to work on your planning skills in the future. Got to dash, another call coming in."

Gillian abruptly disconnected their call.

Ben stared at his phone as if it were some kind of medieval torture device. Then he headed back upstairs, bracing himself for the inevitable chaos.

CHAPTER 49

To his surprise, Ben's apartment was unnaturally quiet. Billy and Lily had stopped running around and were now engrossed in their iPads. Each was wearing headsets, so the adults didn't have to listen to cartoons. Anderson and Molly were making themselves comfortable in his room. Holly and Todd were in the kitchen working on something for dinner for everyone. Caitlin was nowhere to be seen and Sara was sitting in his favorite chair reading a book.

Sara Holcolm grew up in Wallaceton and was known as the prettiest girl in town. She thought of becoming a model or an actress when she was growing up, but a family tragedy changed that. One night, during her senior year in high school, her parents went to a church cookout. One of the parishioners' relatives, visiting from Texas, drank too much beer and got out of control. Some of the men at the cookout tried to restrain him, but he suddenly exploded, pulled a handgun and shot eight people, killing three. Sara's mother and father were among the dead.

From that moment on, Sara's life was profoundly changed. She had no siblings and no other living relatives. Her parents had been deeply in debt so there was little money left to her in their estates. The man who shot them was unemployed and broke, so there was no money that could come in a lawsuit against him.

A couple of families in Wallaceton took her in while she

finished high school, but after that, she had to live on her own and work to pay her bills. Since Wallaceton was such a small town, she moved to Des Moines and lived with a family with Wallaceton roots. She worked as the nanny for their two young children.

Despite her hardship, she applied to Drake University's School of Education. Becoming a teacher seemed like a way she could support herself and lead a productive life by improving the lives of the next generation, and she loved being around kids.

She received a full tuition and board four-year scholarship and graduated at the top of her class. When she moved into the dorm, she took jobs as a barista at Starbucks, she walked dogs, she washed hair in a beauty salon, and she washed dogs at a local groomer's to earn money and save for her future.

With her parents gone and no family, she was having a difficult time knowing where she fit into the world. After graduation from Drake, not knowing where else to go, she applied and was accepted to teach second grade at the local grammar school in Wallaceton. There was something about going home, despite the memory of her family tragedy, that gave her an unexpected feeling of comfort. That feeling was enhanced when she moved back to town. She was embraced by everyone, complimented on her strength in the face of unspeakable tragedy, and her courage. She felt loved and cared for, which was more important to her than working in a big city school system. And working with young children helped to bring out her innate kindness and compassion.

The Wallaces were very aware of the Holcolm tragedy, although they did not know Sara's parents very well. Anderson knew her grandfather from the time he came back from college to take over the family farm. Before they offered her the part-time nanny job over Christmas break, they asked around and everyone only had high praise for the woman Sara had become. This was her first year back in Wallaceton and Anderson was very happy to reconnect with her, especially at this time in her life.

Anderson identified with her, as one orphan to another because of a family tragedy, although he never mentioned it.

In college, Sara spent her time studying and working outside jobs. Going to parties and hooking up didn't feel right to her. She never really had a serious boyfriend since her time with Ben in high school and rejected all the young men who trailed after her because of her beauty. Life had dealt her great beauty and great tragedy. Living both had forced her to realize that she had only herself to depend on. As sweet and kind as she seemed, beneath the surface was a survivor who was proud of how far she had come on her own.

When Sara moved back to Wallaceton, her focus was on teaching and doing a good job at it. Boys didn't cross her mind that often and whenever someone approached her for a date, she reflexively declined. She knew she had a problem with relationships, but she didn't know where to turn for help.

Ben sat down on the couch next to Sara.

"Sara," Ben said softly so the whole room wouldn't be involved in the conversation. "How nice to see you again. It's been a long time."

"It has!"

"I was very sorry to hear about your parents," Ben said. "I really don't know what to say."

"Thank you, Ben. It was very difficult, but I'm still standing," she replied.

"How did you get roped into this trip?"

"Our school ... the one where we first met ... is on Christmas break. And since I've never been to Chicago, when your mom asked me to join them, I thought ... why not have an adventure over Christmas. I liked the idea of their bringing your hometown to you as a kind of reunion since you were too busy to be home for the holidays. I thought that was a really sweet thing to do."

"Mom told me that you taught Second Grade," Ben said.

"I do and I love it. The kids are so open to learning. They are so positive. It's really wonderful."

Ben noticed that Sara's eyes seemed to twinkle when she spoke about her job.

"I have a girlfriend – Gillian – you'll meet her tomorrow," he said, feeling a bit awkward about his past feelings for her. "She's from the East Coast."

"That sounds exciting! I'll look forward to it."

Ben's phone rang. The Caller ID read: GILLIAN.

CHAPTER 50

"My calendar!" Gillian said emphatically as soon as Ben answered his phone.

"I'm on it. Look, why don't I pick you up at 4 tomorrow afternoon and bring you back to my apartment to meet everyone?"

"That sounds alright. Are we going out to dinner? What should I wear? How dressed up will your parents be?"

Ben just shook his head. She clearly did not understand the Wallace family.

"Anything you wear will be fine. You always look great. See you tomorrow."

Ben hung up and looked over at Sara.

"That was Gillian. She's anxious to meet everyone."

"Ben, honey," Molly Wallace said as she came out of his bedroom. "Do you have some extra pillows and maybe another blanket for your dad?"

"Mom," Ben replied, "I'm sorry ... but I can order some from Amazon and they might be able to have them here later tonight."

"No dear, that won't be necessary. You father can get some from the RV. And, honey, what do you have planned for us tomorrow? We'll be up early and eager to see the sights."

I love my family ... I love my family ... Ben kept repeating silently to himself.

CHAPTER 51

It wasn't long before the Wallace clan began to ask about dinner. Holly and Todd were already setting up a buffet since the apartment's dining table could only accommodate four people. When Holly announced that dinner would be eaten picnic-style on the living room floor, Billy and Lily cheered and Ben realized he no longer had any space in the apartment he could call his own.

Part way through the meal, Mackenzie arrived home. Ben introduced her to his family, and she sat down next to Siobhan and Caitlin. He noticed their quick friendship but didn't dwell on it. At least, for the moment, no one was on his case.

After dinner, Mackenzie announced that she was going to bed. She had been on a 24-hour shift at the hospital and was exhausted. Siobhan announced that she was taking Caitlin to the Hubba-Deen Tavern across the street for a beer to celebrate her first trip to Chicago.

As Holly and Todd inflated the air mattresses for everyone and settled their kids down for the night, Sara prepared to read them a bedtime story.

"Ben," Molly said quietly to her son, "while everyone is getting settled, can you come into our room. We want to speak to you in private."

CHAPTER 52

"Ben," his mother began, after she closed the door to his bedroom, "tell us about Siobhan and Mackenzie."

"Well, they are very nice," Ben replied. "It's their loft and I am just a border. I found them through one of the attorneys at work. They keep to themselves and are very nice."

Ben stopped when he realized he was stammering and repeating himself.

"They're gay, aren't they?" Molly asked.

"Yes, Mom, their lesbians. Very common here in the *big* city."

"Are they lovers," she went on.

"Yes, Mom, but they are very quiet about it."

Anderson Wallace sat silently, listening without making any editorial expressions.

"Do they have good jobs?" she asked.

"Look, Mom," Ben replied, a bit on the defensive, "Mackenzie is finishing her training as a surgeon at the University of Chicago. She went to Harvard undergrad and was #2 in her class. She did her medical training at the University of Chicago on a full scholarship.

"Siobhan works in private equity – finance to you and me. She has an undergraduate degree from Sanford and an MBA of the University of Chicago. She was #1 in her class at Sanford.

"They are smart young women who fell in love. And they are respectful of me. End of the interrogation, please."

Ben's father stepped in.

"I've heard enough," he said. "Ben, come with me to the RV to get some blankets. We can talk on the way."

CHAPTER 53

"Ben," Anderson Wallace began as they exited his apartment building and walked through the snow to the Tesla parking lot where the RV was parked. "I don't care about your lifestyle ..."

"Dad," Ben interrupted him, "I am not gay. My roommates are and it is not contagious."

"I understand, Son. What I'm focusing on is your career. I don't see that it is going too well if you have to live in someone else's apartment. I would have thought by now you had come along much farther, especially after doing so well in law school at Northwestern. You talk about your roommates as if they are geniuses. Remember, you graduated with high honors at the very top of your class.

"And your mom and I made sure that you weren't burdened by student loans so that you could build a successful life for yourself in the *big* city."

"It's different," Ben replied. "Look, I'm working 100 hours a week and I'm being considered for partner. I'm well paid, but after taxes, rent, suits, my car and a little entertainment, there's not much left. I'm really grateful for you and mom paying for my education. A lot of my friends and colleagues have huge student debt and it is really crushing their dreams. I'm making my way and if I close this deal on Friday, I think I'll be made partner in the firm next year."

By the time he had finished defending himself, Ben and his father had reached the family RV. When they went inside,

Ben followed his father into the back section. It took his breath away.

"Wow, I guess this is our inheritance," he said.

"None of your business," his father replied.

"Just kidding," Ben said, back-peddling. "This is quite something. It looks like the inside of a fancy yacht."

"Here, help me with the blankets," Anderson said, "and tell me more about this deal on Friday."

"There isn't much more I can tell you. Confidentiality and all that. The Westwoods are like you and mom. Wonderful, kind people."

"Do they have children?"

"No, they said they never had time. Too busy building their business, I guess."

"How do they treat their employees?"

"Like they are family. Really, Dad, they are like hometown, Iowa folk with the right values."

"You never told me about your law firm," Anderson continued. "Are they the same kind of folk?"

"Look, Dad, this is not something you are familiar with. It's different from your friendly country lawyer in Wallaceton. These law firms are very much performance based. Someone called it an 'eat what you kill' world."

"And you are happy in that *world*?"

"I'm making my way. Once I'm a partner, I think it will be different," Ben answered, very much on the defensive.

"It was your choice to be an attorney and your choice to practice in the city. I guess you'll have to sleep in the bed you made for yourself. But your mother is worried about you, so be sensitive with her."

As Anderson Wallace locked up his RV, Ben went to look

at the Tesla SUV hitched to it.

"When did you get a Tesla?" Ben asked.

"It's called a Model X - Plaid. They delivered it two weeks ago. Your mother drives it too fast though."

"Very 21st century. Surprising."

With that, Ben and his father walked back to his apartment in silence, carrying blankets and enjoying the intense quiet the snow had brought.

CHAPTER 54

No sooner had Ben and his father brought the blankets into his bedroom than Molly sat him down to talk about one more subject that was very important to her.

"Ben, honey, you didn't tell us about your special girl."

"Mom, she's great. She's coming over tomorrow afternoon to meet you. She's smart. She's from the East Coast. She wants to get ahead."

Anderson gave Molly a quick glance that Ben did not see.

"Well, we can't wait to meet her," Molly said. "In the meantime, have you spoken with Sara? I think she still likes you from high school."

"Mom," Ben replied with a little edge in his voice, but then caught himself and toned it down, "where is this going?"

"Just asking," she replied. "You never know about things."

"Mom, OK ... and I want to hear about you and your Tesla."

"What do you have planned for us tomorrow," Molly said, changing the subject. "We want to see Chicago and do everything!"

"I'll have to work on it," Ben replied, confident that his Chat GPT artificial intelligence program could come up with a winning itinerary.

CHAPTER 55

Ben spent the rest of the evening catching up with Holly and Todd. They hadn't seen each other in person for almost three years because of the COVID pandemic and the lockdowns, and Holly delighted in showing Ben photos and movies on her phone of the kids growing up.

Holly was the oldest daughter of Anderson and Molly Wallace. Todd came from a farming family in the next town over from Wallaceton. They met in high school and were engaged just after graduation. Todd enlisted in the Marines thereafter and was on his second tour of duty in Afghanistan when he was wounded. He retired from the Marines at the rank of Sergeant with several medals, including a Silver Star for bravery and a Purple Heart when an IED blew his leg apart. As fierce as he could be in the Marines, he was that gentle with his family and friends.

When Todd returned home, because of his war wound, he couldn't continue working on the family farm and was recruited by old man Covington, a World War II marine veteran, to take over his insurance agency in Wallaceton. Covington spent time teaching Todd the business and then retired after arranging a long-term buyout that was favorable for both of them. Although he was a very hard worker, selling insurance was just not Todd's strength, and despite his best efforts, times were tough for he and Holly.

In order to make ends meet, Holly and Todd started baking chocolate chip cookies in their kitchen and selling them on the internet. It wasn't much in the beginning, but their business was slowly growing.

Holly was the personification of a small-town girl with rock solid values and a focus on family. Her positive attitude toward life was reflected in her love of Todd and in her two children, Billy (age 10) and Lily (age 7). No matter how challenging the circumstance, Holly always looked for the goodness in people.

Around 10:30, Ben made himself comfortable on one of the single air mattresses and immediately fell into a deep sleep. It was the sound of a dozen police sirens that woke him up.

He went to the front window of his apartment and saw a crowd of officers standing outside the Hubba-Deen Tavern across the street. He hoped his sister and Siobhan hadn't gotten themselves into the middle of something. When he saw a local NBC news truck pull up, he called Siobhan's cell phone.

"I'm looking out of the window at the commotion in front of the Hubba-Deen. You guys aright? Do you need emergency legal counsel?" Ben asked.

"Ha, ha," Siobhan replied over the noise from the bar, "Caitlin and I can take care of ourselves. See you later."

With that, Ben went back to sleep and didn't give the incident another thought. It wasn't until the next day that events at the Hubba-Deen came into focus for the entire Wallace family.

CHAPTER 56

Billy and Lily were up early. Very early. And they were ready to go.

"Uncle Ben," they shouted as they jumped on his air mattress, waking him up. "What are we going to do today?"

Ben rubbed his eyes open, pulled up the Chat GPT app on his phone and scanned its suggestions.

"Well, today, for the girls, I thought you, Lily, your mom, Caitlin, Granny and Sara would go shopping and to The American Girl Place ..."

"Yippee!" she squealed in delight.

"And for the boys, Billy, I thought you, your dad, Grandpa and me would go to the Museum of Science and Industry where we can see a real, actual submarine that was captured during World War II and see the IMAX movie about Volcanoes."

"Yippee!" Billy shouted.

"Cool, huh," Ben added for good measure.

His phone suddenly rang. The Caller ID read: NED MARTIN.

Ben told the kids he had an important call, and he went into the powder room to take it.

"Mr. Martin ..."

"Be in my office at 9am," Martin demanded.

"Sir, I'm ... sorry ... I have a prior engagement ... " Ben replied, beginning to feel his heart starting to race, "... but I can work around it. I'll be there. Of course. Is this about the Westwood deal?"

"Just get in here."

Ned Martin abruptly ended the call.

Ben's mind was going a mile-a-minute as he quickly got dressed.

CHAPTER 57

Before he left for the office, Ben organized everyone's day. He left written directions and a map to Michigan Avenue for shopping, The American Girl Place and where to park for his mom, and he left a note for his dad that he had to run to the office for a short meeting and would be back by 10:30am to pick them up to go to the museum.

Because of the storm, he had to dig his car out of the snow. It took him way too long.

Walking into Ned Martin's office at 9:05am, Ben thought he was ready for whatever happened overnight. The full force hit him as he sat down.

"Wallace, what have you done?" Ned Martin shouted.

"I honestly don't know, Sir," Ben replied calmly.

"TECH-AI's attorney called me to tell me, as a courtesy no less, that he is filling a bar complaint against you for violating ethical rules."

"What?"

"I don't know the full extent of the problem," Martin continued, "but it is going to reflect very badly on this firm and, of course, our clients."

"With all due respect," Ben replied, keeping his composure, "I think this is a bargaining tactic. I have done absolutely nothing wrong. I have not violated any ethical rules. My gut tells me that we need to ignore this bluster and see if these guys come to the closing tomorrow as planned. My clients are fine with that. If Dunn wants to file against me, let him. I'll deal with it."

Ned Martin quietly thought through Ben's response.

"Alright, Wallace, it's your head. Do it your way, but if this deal doesn't close on time, consider yourself fired."

"Understood," Ben said, rose from his chair and walked out of Martin's office, privately thanking his lucky stars that he had clients like the Westwoods.

Ben arrived back at his apartment a little before 10. The girls had already left for their adventures.

"Ready, Gentlemen?" Ben asked as he gathered the "boys" for their expedition to the Museum, the only place on earth where they could visit the depths of the ocean and fly over active volcanoes without leaving Chicago.

CHAPTER 58

Everyone returned to Ben's apartment around 3pm that afternoon. Lily was so excited by her trip to The American Girl Place that she had to tell her father, then her grandfather and then Ben all about her adventure. And, she had to show each of them the doll that Granny had bought for her and the clothes, shoes, books and other American Girl essentials.

"I'll bet that set you back some," Ben whispered to his mother.

"It was wonderful to see her face light up," Molly replied. "It was an experience that she will always remember. And Michigan Avenue had so many beautiful holiday decorations and lights in the trees. It was such fun."

Since Lily made the rounds recounting her day, Billy was not about to be left out. He went to his mother, grandmother and Aunt Caitlin and told them that he saw a World War II submarine and watched real volcanoes erupting.

And then he told them about the Whispering Gallery where your quietest voice could be heard clear across a room and how amazing it was.

Ben's phone rang. The Caller ID read: GILLIAN.

"Are you coming for me?" she asked.

Ben realized that he had forgotten to pick her up.

"Twenty minutes ... I'll be right over. Be downstairs in your lobby."

Ben excused himself and told everyone to get ready to meet his girlfriend.

CHAPTER 59

The ride back to Ben's apartment with Gillian was frosty, to say the least. She made no bones about feeling left out and did not hide her displeasure.

"Everyone, this is Gillian," Ben announced as he escorted her into his living room and then made the introductions. When they reached Ben's parents, his mother spoke first.

"So nice to meet you, Gillian," Molly began. "Ben tells me that you are from the East Coast. What brought you to Chicago?"

Gillian put on a polite smile but seeing Ben's father in his farmer overalls and his mother dressed in an oversized, knitted sweater devoid of style, closed the book on his family for her. If Ben was going to accompany her on her climb to the top of Chicago society, he would have to push his family far into the background. The Wallaces were clearly not "her" kind of people and she wondered how Ben had managed to escape his ancestral handicap.

"I felt that Chicago had opportunities for me," Gillian responded. "I saw it as a place where I could be an influencer for good."

Anderson Wallace stood stone-faced.

"That's nice," Molly said. "What exactly is an 'influencer for good,' dear?"

Gillian's expression did not hide her frustration with these backwater hicks.

"Oh, think of it as someone who takes a leadership role at a certain level of society and tells people how to think and how things should be."

Ben listened to her response and cringed. This was not going well.

CHAPTER 60

In the background, someone had turned the living room television to a local news channel to check the weather report. To everyone's surprise, the first local story was about a young woman who fought off three attackers, single-handedly, at a tavern in the Fulton Market area the night before.

"Caitlin Wallace, a Mixed Martial Arts instructor from Iowa, in Chicago for the Christmas holiday ...," the news anchor began.

There was a hush in the room as all eyes turned to Caitlin.

"This young woman," the anchor continued, "was attacked by three men in their twenties who were trying to rob the tavern and the patrons. According to the police report, when the men demanded Caitlin's cell phone, she just took them down ... in less than twenty seconds. Two of the would-be robbers suffered broken legs and concussions, and the third suffered three broken ribs, a broken arm and a cracked collar bone."

"What made you do this?" a young, female reporter asked Caitlin at the scene.

"I did what needed to be done," she replied.

Standing behind Caitlin, Siobhan could be seen beaming.

As the news report wrapped up, Molly went over to her daughter and gave her a hug.

"Honey, are you alright?"

"Of course, Mom. I was ready to do a lot more to these guys, but they just gave up and I throttled back."

Off in the corner, no one noticed the look of pride on Anderson Wallace's face.

"She was a hero," Siobhan said. "I guess men need to think twice before messing with strong, independent women."

Ben was finally getting the drift about his sister who was the middle child between he and Holly.

Caitlin was born six weeks early, fighting for life, and it was a quality that she displayed from her earliest days through today.

Always feeling like an outcast in high school, and not understanding why, Caitlin's inner turmoil often emerged in a combination of rage and retreat. Her temper was legendary during her teenage years, and it was usually followed by periods of withdrawal from everything. Anderson and Molly had their hands full with her moodiness and her hostility to traditional family activities.

At college, however, Caitlin seemed to find herself and calm down. In fact, she discovered that preferred the company and companionship of women to men and that she was a lesbian. Although she never "came out" to her parents and hid her sexual orientation from the rest of her family, by graduation from college, she knew who she was to become.

One day, in her senior year at the Iowa State, a friend took her to a martial arts studio to pick up her younger brother. Something connected for Caitlin the second she walked into the dojo. Whether it was smell, the lighting, the quiet, there was a feeling that told her she wanted to be there.

From that day forward, Caitlin began her martial arts journey and over the next three years, she earned her Professional Mixed Martial Arts Instructor's Certificate. Her gifted agility, her innate competitiveness and her birthright instinct to fight made her a natural for the MMA sport. Rather than compete professionally, even though she was good enough, she chose to instruct so that she could lead a more normal life.

While she was earning her instructor's certificate, she lived in Ames, Iowa, worked any job she could find and had several steamy relationships with girls she met at and after college.

When Caitlin came to Chicago on the family Christmas reunion, she had mixed emotions. Being with the family for that long a time, in such close quarters, looked like it would be torture. However, since she hadn't seen her older sister and her brother in years, she let her mother talk her into the trip.

CHAPTER 61

"Who wants pizza?" Ben shouted above the din of congratulations to Caitlin in his living room.

"Meeee!" Lily squealed.

"Meeee!" Billy shouted.

"I know you had pizza two nights ago in Springfield," Ben said to his sister Holly, "but you can't visit Chicago without having our famous deep-dish pizza. It's world famous. Is it alright for the kids?"

"Of course," she responded. "Whatever you want."

"Then Chicago-style pizza it is!" he announced.

With that Ben excused himself and went into his bedroom to place the order on his computer.

Gillian followed.

"Ben, I can't stay," she said as she nervously paced from wall-to-wall.

"Why?" he asked.

"I'm not very good with situations like this. Take me home, please."

Ben was surprised at her request, but he was more surprised that he didn't want to try to change her mind. From the look on Gillian face, it was obvious that his family was a non-starter with her and a barrier to her ambitions. Being rude to them clearly didn't matter to her.

"If that's what you want ..." Ben said as he shrugged his shoulders. "As soon as I complete the pickup order from

Pizzeria Duo, we'll be on our way."

"You can tell everyone that I was not feeling well and needed to go home," she suggested.

"Sure ... sure," Ben replied.

Back in the living room Ben shouted, "I'll be back in about an hour," and walked out of the apartment with Gillian following a few steps behind him.

CHAPTER 62

The ride to Gillian's apartment building was uncomfortable. Her behavior was something he had not seen before, and it was not acceptable in his book. There was a lot that Ben wanted to say, but he didn't want to get into it while he was navigating through the snowy streets.

"Ben," Gillian began when they reached her building, "I really liked you, but I can't have in-laws like that. They just aren't in my plan. I feel like you've wasted my time. Have a nice life."

With that, she stepped out of the car without giving him a chance to say anything and slammed the door behind her.

Ben sat in silence as he watched her walk into the lobby of her apartment building and into one of the elevators. He felt sad to lose her, but glad he found out before their relationship got much more serious.

City girls are just not country girls, he thought to himself.

He turned the car radio on, Bluetoothed his Spotify playlist from his phone and let Blake Shelton's *No Body* transport him to back to the world of his roots as he drove to pick up the pizzas.

CHAPTER 63

The Wallace family devoured the four Chicago-style pizzas that Ben brought home. The thick crust, tangy sauce and gooey cheese was a big hit with everyone.

"The best we've ever had," Molly proclaimed. "Nothing like this in Wallaceton. We'll have to come back to Chicago, just for the pizza!"

The conversation during dinner was all about Caitlin's confrontation in the bar the night before. Everyone wanted to know every detail, again and again. She was a real-life hero and famous now that she had been on TV.

Ben's phone chimed with a text while everyone was engrossed in Siobhan's blow-by-blow account.

The text was from Attorney Dunn. It read: "Wallace, we have uncovered some shady accounting done by the Westwoods. If this isn't cleared up by tomorrow morning, the deal is off."

The text offered no details, just allegations and threats.

Ben's face reflected his frustration with the circumstances.

His father noticed and pulled him aside to a far corner of the living room.

"Tough time with this deal?" he asked.

"Dad, you know that dog in the junkyard back home that always had a bad attitude, all the time, and just kept looking for an opportunity to bite someone. Well, this attorney, on the other side of my deal, makes that dog look like a happy puppy."

Anderson Wallace put his hand on his son's shoulder.

"Things have a tendency of working out," he said.

"I hope so, Dad, I hope so."

CHAPTER 64

Once Billy and Lily drifted off to sleep, Sara came over to the corner where Ben was working on his laptop and sat down on the floor next to him.

"I hope Gillian feels better," Sara said quietly.

"Thanks, but we hit a speed bump or a brick wall or something. We're over. I don't really want to get into it."

Sara immediately changed the subject.

"Your mom, Holly, Caitlin and, of course, Lily had a really nice day, especially at The American Girl Place."

"Some of the attorneys at the law firm talked about taking their daughters there. It's supposed to be one of the highlights of Chicago."

"I'll let you in on a secret," Sara said, "if you want."

"Sure. I can keep a secret."

Ben leaned closer to her.

"I've always dreamed of visiting that place," Sara began, "ever since I was a little girl. I had one American Girl doll and clothes and even an American Girl kitchen, with an over, a refrigerator and a stove. Oh, and books, too. My family didn't have a lot of money and they thought it was quite extravagant of me. I guess I've always been a bit of a dreamer."

"Sara, I've always liked that quality about you, from the very first time we met in high school. Your secret is safe with me."

"Thank you," she said, with a slight blush in her cheeks.

"Now, please forgive me, but I've got this big closing tomorrow and I've got a mountain of things to review."

"Of course, I understand. I hope it all goes well for you," she said and moved over to her air mattress near the kids.

Ben decided to ignore Attorney Dunn's threatening, last minute text and call his bluff by letting the text go unanswered.

CHAPTER 65

Just as Ben was beginning to drift off to sleep, his sister Holly came over and sat down next to his air mattress.

"Benny," she said in a very quiet voice so that she didn't wake her children, "I'm sorry we haven't had a chance to catch up. I can see how much pressure you are under. Is there anything I can do to help?"

"Sis, nice of you," Ben replied as he yawned, "but no. Nothing. I've got to plough my way through. Mom told me that you and Todd started a cookie business out of your kitchen. How is that going?"

Holly's mouth widened into a big smile.

"Well, very well. I guess people like our chocolate chip oatmeal cookies. All natural ingredients, of course."

"Cool! Happy for you," Ben replied. "Tell me, how is it still living in Wallaceton with mom and dad so close by? I know it's a small town, but doesn't that make it even smaller?"

"They are a big help, mom more than dad, of course. They do save us money on babysitting. We're on a tight budget, but making ends meet, and we're proud of it."

"Any thoughts on that dinosaur RV? What has been going through dad's head? And a super-fast Tesla? Who are our parents turning into? I guess there won't be much left of the family farm if they keep spending like this. But they seem happy."

"Benny, we don't say anything. And you know dad, he

doesn't say much either. All I know is that Todd and I are happy."

"You are doing a wonderful job with Billy and Lily. They are terrific kids. Positive, enthusiastic, curious and respectful. Everything we all weren't growing up," Ben replied.

"They are. They are the next generation of Wallaces, and we want them to be the best generation yet!"

"Sis, you'll pardon me, but I've got to get some sleep. Tomorrow is going to be a bear of a day for me. Loved that you came over to talk though."

CHAPTER 66

Ben was up before 5am. He quietly shaved, showered and dressed without waking his parents, who were fast asleep in his bed.

Quietly, he crept through the living room, careful not to wake the rest of his family, out the front door and into his car. The weather had cleared. To his relief, his car had not been ploughed under by the city. He considered it a good omen.

He thought about stopping for a Starbuck's, but his stomach was calling the shots and it was filled with nerves. In ten minutes, he was in the office's parking garage.

Everything at the law firm was dark and quiet. He was the first one in.

Only a few more hours until this deal is closed, he said to himself, as he started to mentally prepare for the confrontation certain to be ahead.

When he reached his desk, he saw the message light on his phone silently blinking.

CHAPTER 67

Ben played the phone message that was left overnight. It was from the Westwoods' accounting firm. They were confirming that they would be available for a Zoom at 1pm, ready to respond to any questions at the closing.

Ben nodded. So far, so good.

He went into the firm's kitchen, made a strong cup of coffee and spent a few minutes envisioning the different ways the day might play out.

Back at his desk, his attention was riveted to his computer when Neil Martin unexpectedly walked in.

"Wallace, I just wanted to know if you need some help with this closing ..." Martin suggested.

Ben wasn't immediately sure how to interpret his boss' intentions.

"Mr. Martin, are you doubting my work or my ability to get this done?"

"Not exactly, but since this is your first major deal, and you know how important it is for the firm, I just wanted to offer my assistance."

"I am aware of the significance," Ben replied. "However, and with all due respect, if one of the senior partners of this firm suddenly inserts himself into the closing, I'm afraid that my effectiveness and my credibility will be destroyed. Counsel for the buyers has been vigorously looking for an opening to gain leverage and this could not only put the deal at risk, but also hurt our clients. If this deal doesn't close, a major lawsuit between the parties is guaranteed, and if our clients are at fault, it could cost them millions. So, again, with all due respect, I would appreciate your faith in my abilities and permit me to do my job."

"Well, Wallace, as my brother told you, this is your make-or-break moment. Good luck to you."

Neil Martin spun on his heals, turned his back to Ben and walked out of his office.

Suddenly Ben's earlier good omen was not looking so good.

CHAPTER 68

After his encounter with Neil Martin, Ben began to wonder what circle of Dante's Hell he was currently trapped in. His query was interrupted when his secretary, Jessie, arrived for work.

Jessie had been Ben's secretary for the three and a half years he had worked at Martin & Martin. She was about eight years older than he was, not married and lived with two cats. She had been married in her twenties, but her husband became a drug addict and overdosed on their living room couch. Since then, she has avoided relationships with men and found a circle of women she could depend on. She looked at Ben as a younger brother and was always thinking ahead for his best interests.

"Ben," Jessie began, "I have all the documents you emailed me last night and they ready to go."

"Great. We need five sets of originals," Ben replied.

"That's my next task. I came in early to take some of the pressure off you," she said with a smile.

"Very thoughtful of you. I've been thinking of how I want to stage the closing. Let's put Mr. and Mrs. Westwood on the far side of the conference table, with their backs to the windows. The buyers and Dunn will be directly across from them. I'll sit next to Mrs. Westwood.

"Please see that someone from the kitchen staff has bottles of water, soda, a thermos of coffee and mini-chocolate biscuits on the credenza. China cups and saucers – not the paper to-go cups. Cloth napkins and small china plates with the firm's logo for the biscuits. And a ball point pen and a law firm logo pad at each place. I want this closing to be set up so that people feel a sense organization and formality."

Ben had been to numerous closings at the firm, but only a few stood out in setting the right tone. Since this was going to be the biggest moment in his legal career, he wanted to do it the right way.

CHAPTER 69

Ben's phone rang. The Caller ID read: MOM. He let it go to voicemail. When the recording was over, he listened to it.

"Hi, Honey, it's Mom. You left so early this morning. And so quietly too. I wanted to let you know that we are planning to take everyone out for dinner tonight to celebrate your big deal. Your roommate Siobhan is going to make a reservation for all of us at the best steak restaurant in Chicago. Your roommates are so nice! We invited them, too. See you later, dear."

His mother's message only served to crank up his level of stress yet another notch. Of course, no one had asked for his opinion, and to plan a celebratory dinner for a deal that was not done yet, seemed a lot like tempting fate.

Since everything he could do was done, Ben spent the next few hours ploughing through paperwork on other matters that had built up over the past week. Changing his focus from the Westwood's deal actually helped to bring some calm to his day, however temporary.

CHAPTER 70

Betty and Arnold Westwood arrived at Ben's law firm at 12:30pm, half an hour before the closing was to start. Ben had Jessie usher them into the conference room where he met them a few minutes later. She had offered them refreshments, but they had declined.

"Big day," Ben said as he entered the room. "How are you both doing?"

"You know, Ben," Betty Westwood replied, "this is a great moment for us, but it is still a bittersweet. We have given our hearts and souls, and our lives, to this company. It is time, however, for us to work on accomplishing our next goal."

Arnold Westwood was clearly not as calm as his wife. He found it difficult to keep seated at the long table and kept getting up and walking around the room, looking out the window or consulting his iPhone.

"Arnold," Ben said, "I know this is an important passage in your lives and I have done everything in my power to help you preserve your legacies."

"I know, Ben," he replied, "I know. You have worked very diligently on our behalf. I know this is the right thing to do. And at the right time. We can do so much good."

"Yes," Betty agreed. "Ben once this sale is closed, since we don't have any children, we want all the money to go into a foundation that will pay the college tuition for deserving young people interested in the sciences. Can you help us do that?"

"Of course," Ben responded. "I'd be honored."

"Ben," Arnold interjected, "I just can't get my arms around trusting these buyers. There's something not right. I just can't put my finger on it."

It was 12:55pm. Five minutes before the closing was to begin and the buyers had not yet arrived. Ben looked at his phone. No messages. No texts. Nothing from Charles Dunn.

CHAPTER 71

The tension in the law firm's conference room grew with every passing minute.

Finally, at 1:35pm, two young Gen Z'ers, dressed in hoodies and sweatpants, arrived with Attorney Dunn. They marched into the room in an aggressive, hostile manner.

"Welcome," Ben said, as he directed them where to sit.

Dunn, however, wasted no time. "Wallace, my clients think your clients have intentionally mispriced the intellectual property rights held by the Westwood's company. They have reached the conclusion that the patents are not worth what we've been told. In fact, they think the Westwoods have grossly overvalued and inflated the values in a way that borders on civil and, maybe, even criminal fraud."

Charles Dunn was on his feet. Staring directly at the Westwoods. Accusing them to their faces. His manner was belligerent and threatening.

Ben jumped to his feet, looked over at Betty and Arnold, and then confronted Dunn head-on.

"Look, Mr. Dunn, you are making very serious allegations and I can assure you they are completely unfounded. This deal was fully negotiated over months and your clients had plenty of time to do their due diligence. They had plenty of time to bring this or any issue of valuation to the table, well in advance of today. Your clients could have pulled out of this deal at multiple times along the way, without any penalty to them, if they were not satisfied with anything.

"We are here today," Ben continued, "at the culmination of a very long, extensive and expensive negotiation and now you come in here at the very last minute and try to blow it up. If this is your way of throwing your weight around in an attempt to renegotiate the price, let us know right now, or sit down."

Ben was not about to let Dunn get away with these terrorist tactics.

"Now, you will please excuse us" Ben announced, "while I speak with my clients in private."

Ben escorted the Westwood out of the conference room and down the long hall to his office where they could talk in private.

CHAPTER 72

"Betty ... Arnold," Ben said somberly when they reached his office and he had shut the door. "I am so sorry. These people just keep pushing, trying to intimidate you and force the price down. Of course, it's up to you. I'll do whatever you want."

"Ben," Betty replied, "you know us. We are straightshooters and we prize honesty, honor and doing the right thing. If we say this deal is over, how much will it cost us to walk away?"

Arnold was nodding in agreement to his wife's words, as he paced around Ben's small office.

"If these guys are prepared to sign the fully negotiated and agreed to deal in front of them, and you aren't, I'm afraid you will incur a million-dollar forfeiture penalty."

"And if they walk out?" Betty asked.

"If they don't close, then they will forfeit a million dollars. Of course, this will certainly result in them filling litigation accusing you of fraud, and maybe worse, and tying-up your company for years," Ben responded.

"So be it," Betty said. "Arnold?"

"I'm in!" he exclaimed.

Ben's respect for Betty and Arnold's grit, character and values energized him for the next step.

"Ready?" Ben said as he motioned to his office door.

"Ready!" Betty responded. "We're with you, Ben. Give 'em hell!"

CHAPTER 73

Ben led Betty and Arnold Westwood back into the conference room. They took their seats and Ben began.

"Mr. Dunn, are your buyers ready to execute the closing documents before you, at the price and terms fully negotiated, or not?" Ben asked in a firm and clear voice.

"Wallace, you are too young and too inexperienced to get it. Your people breached the agreement and, unless they are willing to take a lesser price, my clients have instructed me to file suit immediately."

Dunn rose to his feet.

"You have screwed your clients, Wallace, and if we find that you participated in the fraud, I'll have your license revoked, too!"

The two young tech wizards in their hoodies nodded their agreement in unison. Their bobbing heads, inside the oversized hoodies, reminded Ben of the dwarfs from *Snow White*.

Ben slowly rose to his feet and pointed directly at Dunn.

"Mr. Dunn, clients stand ready, willing and able to sign the agreement before you," Ben said. "If your client's refuse, so be it. We can sort out their penalty and damages in court ... if that is what you prefer. The ball is in your court. It's time to put up or shut up ... Sir."

With that the conference room door opened and Jessie rushed in, completely flustered.

CHAPTER 74

"Ben, I'm so sorry," Jessie said, as she raced over to him, "I don't mean to burst into your closing, but you have visitors. They won't take 'NO' for an answer when I tell them you are in a meeting and can't be disturbed."

Just as she finished, Anderson and Molly Wallace marched into the conference room. Anderson was wearing his signature farmer's overalls and Molly was dressed in an oversized knitted sweater. They looked exactly like who they were – farmers from Iowa.

"Mom ... Dad ... what are you doing here? I'm in the middle of a closing. You can't be in here. Can we take this outside, please?"

Ben turned to the Westwoods and then to Dunn.

"I'm sorry for the interruption."

Anderson Wallace sat down at the head of the long conference table and motioned for Molly to sit next to Betty Westwood.

"I understand you are interested in selling your company," he said, directly to the Westwoods, "and these kids over here are giving you a hard time, trying to steal it at a discount. Have I got it right?"

"Dad," Ben said nervously, "this is just so out of order and inappropriate. Can we talk about it later? Will you and mom please leave?"

"Ben," Anderson replied, in no uncertain terms, "take a seat."

Anderson then turned his attention to Dunn and his two hooded clients.

"What are you fellas up to?"

"Mr. Wallace, you need to leave this meeting right now!" Dunn exclaimed, pointing his long index finger at the conference room door. "You are interfering with a business contract," Dunn continued, "and you are going to cause a lot of financial damage to your son's clients and to your son. Do you really want to be responsible for that?"

Dunn looked hostile and threatening as he stood directly in front of Ben's father.

Anderson Wallace, however, ignored him and looked over to Betty Westwood.

"How much are you asking for your company?" he asked.

"First, Mr. Wallace, how nice to meet Ben's parents. He is a wonderful young man. You have much to be proud of. As for our deal, it is for $250 million in cash."

Anderson turned his attention back to Dunn and his two clients.

"This meeting is over for you. You three can go."

CHAPTER 75

Ben didn't understand what was happening except that he had lost control of the meeting as Dunn and his clients stormed out of the conference room, with Dunn shouting, "See you in court!"

"We're looking forward to it!" Arnold shouted back, with his fist in the air and a big smile on his face.

When they had left, Anderson leaned forward to be closer to the Westwoods.

"Mrs. Westwood ... Betty ... and Arnold," Anderson said quietly, I'll buy your company for what you are asking. Is that alright?"

Ben listened to the words coming out of his father's mouth and felt like his head was going to explode. His father was acting like a crazy man, living in a delusional world. How could he be saying these things? He had just blown up the Westwoods' deal at the cost of millions in penalties and litigation costs, and destroyed his son's legal career, all in the space of three minutes.

CHAPTER 76

Ben knew that his career at Martin & Martin had just flat-lined. By five o'clock, they would be handing him a pink slip and telling him to clean out his desk. A Christmas "present" that he would always remember.

"Tell me, Betty," Anderson went on, "would you mind if I made a few adjustments to our deal?"

Betty and Arnold looked puzzled.

"I would like to buy your company for the full $250 million in cash," Anderson explained, "but I would also like to include further payments to you of 10% of the royalties earned by Arnold's existing patents for the duration of those patents, plus 25% of the royalties earned from future patents that Arnold receives that can be used in the business. Is that alright? And we'll cover any costs and damages if you get sued by those two guys we just kicked out."

Betty looked at Arnold, their surprise evident. They both nodded the agreement.

"However, there is one further condition that Molly and I have," Anderson continued, "we would like to bring Ben into this business, and we would like you to stay on for one year to teach him how to run it. He would become the CEO thereafter. Is that something that you would be willing to do?"

Ben felt that he was living in a parallel universe where his fate was being determined by others, right in front of him, and where he had no power to intervene or even express an opinion.

CHAPTER 77

Betty looked over at Arnold.

"It would be our pleasure," she told Ben's parents. "We think the world of Ben and he will be a perfect fit."

"Dad," Ben interrupted. "This is insane. Where are you and mom going to get $250 million in cash? You are apple farmers from central Iowa. Have I lost my mind or am I living on another planet?"

Molly decided that it was her turn.

"Well, Ben," she began, "there are some things you don't know about your father and me."

She turned to Betty and Arnold.

"It is true that we are farmers on the Wallace farm in Wallaceton, Iowa, that has been in Anderson's family for generations. Our apples are grown and picked with love and care. We are very proud of them."

Ben was holding his head in his hands.

"Along the way," she continued turning back to Ben, "your father and I did some investing, and we made some money that we can use to buy the Westwoods' company and give you a better life than being an attorney at this firm."

Ben raised his head from his hands.

"Some money?" Ben asked.

"Yes, Honey," Molly went on, "your dad looked online this morning and our holdings in Apple stock are worth just over $1 billion dollars."

There was complete silence in the conference room.

"Honey, we are, after all, apple farmers," she added.

The expressions on the Westwoods faces were ones of pride for what the Wallace family had achieved.

Ben, however, was in shock.

CHAPTER 78

"I guess that explains that dinosaur RV you are driving," Ben said as he shook his head slowly back and forth, trying to process all that had happened in the past few minutes.

"Betty," Anderson said, "I spoke with Tim Cook, the CEO of Apple, about your company. Tim is a great friend. We have known him since he joined Apple in 1998. Steve Jobs told us all about him. He has been to our home for dinner, and, on a few occasions, he has secretly come by to help with the apple harvest. He says it relaxes him.

"Anyway," Anderson continued, "Tim explained your company to me and its value in the marketplace. He was very familiar with the brilliant products invented by Arnold and knew all about your patents. He also told me how well-respected you both were in the industry and how you were always there to help others."

Everyone in the conference room was listening intently.

"Tim also agreed to help going forward. Apple will contract with your company to integrate your battery-saver technology into some of their products, and if, after a test period, everything works as expected, then Apple will invest $250 million into the expansion of your factory in Springfield, Illinois. Keeping great products in the U.S. of A. is the right thing to do. Tim was also very impressed with the fact that your factory is carbon neutral today. That is one of Apple's big goals for the coming years.

"If you agree to our two conditions that we pay you royalties on Arnold's current and future patents and that you teach Ben the business, then we are all set and your family will be able to benefit for generations to come," Anderson concluded. "We can have the cash here by Tuesday and finish up."

"Anderson," Betty replied. "We have one condition of our own."

It was the Wallaces' turn to lean forward in their chairs.

"Arnold and I have no children and no living relatives," Betty continued. "As a consequence, we will be setting up a foundation with the proceeds from this sale with a mission to pay the college tuition for young people interested in becoming scientists and inventors. We have mentioned this to Ben. However, it is our condition that Ben joins the Board of Directors of our foundation and that he takes over running it after we are gone."

Ben knew he was hearing words coming out of Betty's mouth, and there was something more about his future, but his brain was just shorting out. The only thing that was clear to him was that his parents and the Westwoods were like peas in a pod.

"That sounds wonderful," Molly responded. "So thoughtful of you to want to help so many young people. I know Ben will be great at it. He is so caring and responsive to the needs of others."

"Science is the future of America and someone has to make sure really smart, dedicated kids, no matter their background, get a shot," Arnold added, holding up his hand to make the victory "V" with his fingers.

"Honey," Molly continued, turning her attention to Ben, "you'll be moving to Springfield. You can stay with Aunt

Katherine until you get settled. Now why don't you go tell your senior partners that you quit, and we will visit with Betty and Arnold."

"And, son, if these fancy Chicago lawyers make a fuss about how this deal turned out for them financially, don't give it a second thought," Anderson added. "We'll make it right by them."

CHAPTER 79

Ben slowly rose from his seat at the conference table, put the fountain pen his Aunt Katherine had given him when he graduated law school into the inner pocket of his suit coat and walked out of the room. His entire future had been rewritten in fifteen minutes and his brain was trying to process what had happened. Like a robot, he followed the instructions he had been given by his mother and walked into Neil Martin's office.

"Mr. Martin," he began in a flat tone, "I regret to inform you that the Westwoods' deal didn't close and that I am hereby submitting my resignation."

Before Martin could respond, Ben turned and started to walk out of his office.

"Wallace!" Martin shouted. "What the ... what happened?"

"The buyers kept changing the deal and the Westwoods were ready to walk. Then my parents arrived and offered to buy their company."

"I'm sorry, but I don't understand," Martin said. "I thought your people were backwoods farmers."

"I'm not sure I do either. It turns out to be complicated. But my father said that he would take care of the law firm's fees, not to worry. My family always does the right thing."

With that, Ben walked out of Neil Martin's office and headed back to the Conference Room.

"Honey," Molly said as Ben entered, "Betty and Arnold are joining us for dinner tonight. Is that great!"

"Yes, of course," Ben said as he collected his papers. He felt like he was moving through some sort of weird Zombie dream as he headed to his office.

"Jessie, I want to say goodbye. I am leaving the firm immediately," Ben announced when he reached his secretary's desk.

The look of surprise on her face was unmistakable.

"Ben ... what happened?"

"I'm not really sure," he replied as he tossed the few personal possessions he had on his desk into his big, brown leather legal bag. "I think I'm giving up the practice of law. At least, that's what it sounded like."

Jessie went over to him and gave him a big hug.

"You have always been so kind and fair to me," she said. "I will always remember you and hope that good things are ahead for you."

"And for you, too," he added before catching up with his parents who were waiting for him by the elevators.

CHAPTER 80

Without really giving it a second thought, Ben rode home with his parents in their Tesla. He was so stunned by the turn of events that he forgot he had driven to work and that his car was in the public garage. He was brought back to reality witnessing his mother drive way too fast through city traffic. From his vantage point in the back seat, every turn she made seemed to be a prelude to a near-death experience.

"Dad," Ben said, between gasps after one close call, then another, "I've got to ask. You said you called a guy about where to park your RV in Chicago. Who did you call?"

Anderson responded off-handedly, without turning around to look at his son.

"I just called Elon and he said that it would not be a problem. He set it up while we were on the phone."

"This is crazy!" Ben exclaimed. "You know Elon Musk? How?"

Molly silently beamed as she listened and drove right through a stop sign.

CHAPTER 81

Back at Ben's apartment, Anderson called his family together for a family meeting.

"Your mother and I wanted to fill you all in on today's happenings," Anderson began as everyone took seats in the living room. "We went to visit Ben at his office, and we met some very nice people, Betty and Arnold Westwood. You will get to meet them tonight at dinner.

"The upshot of our meeting," Anderson continued, "is that your mom and I bought a high-tech company that Ben is going to learn how to run and eventually take over. He is going to be moving to Springfield next week and living at Aunt Katherine's while he gets his feet wet."

The look of shock on Ben's face at the rapid timeline of his new life was not lost on his siblings, who were actually very pleased for him. They had known for a long time that he was not truly happy in the big city.

"Now, since we are doing this for Ben," Anderson continued, "we are going to be doing the following for Holly and Caitlin."

Sara raised her hand.

"Mr. Wallace, since this is your family meeting, would you like me to take the dogs for a walk?"

"Sara, honey," Molly replied, "you just keep your seat. We think of you as part of our family."

"Holly, I spoke to my friend at Walmart," Anderson said, resuming his announcements, "and they are going to start stocking your chocolate chip cookies. They are going to do a test run in three stores in Iowa and if the customers like them, Walmart will do a national deal with you."

It was Holly's turn to be shocked by the turn of events in her life.

"If all goes according to plan, your mother and I will pay to build a state-of-the-art baking factory for you in Wallaceton, and we will help you hire the staff necessary to meet the national orders."

Holly looked over at Todd. They were in disbelief.

"And, Caitlin," Anderson went on, "your mom and I will support your endeavors in every way we can. We want you to know how proud of you we are, and we are prepared to invest in whatever business you want to go into. If you would like to move to Chicago and take over Ben's lease or get your own apartment, we are all for it. And, if you want to establish an MMA gym here in Chicago, we will make it happen. You just have to let us know."

The look on Caitlin's face was priceless. In a matter of only a few seconds, the words from her father made her feel validated and wanted, two things she had secretly hoped for, for years.

"How is all this possible?" Holly asked. "You and mom have always taught us to be so frugal and made us feel that money was always tight."

CHAPTER 82

It was Molly's turn to carry on with the announcements.

"Your father and I have been very fortunate investors," she began, "and we have, over our lifetimes, accumulated quite a bit of money. You are all such great kids. We are so proud of you and of how you turned out that we thought it was about time to improve your lives."

Anderson nodded his head in agreement.

"You all have character, compassion, empathy and are very responsible with money," Molly continued. "But most of all, you know right from wrong, and you each always try to do the right thing. How could parents be anything but proud!"

Ben piped up first. "There's more than just the $1 billion in Apple stock?"

The look of surprise on Holly and Caitlin's faces reached a new level. They had no idea what Ben was talking about.

Molly went on.

"Well, in addition to the Apple stock, there's the Tesla holdings that are worth about $250 million ..."

"And that's how you know Elon Musk?" Ben asked, interrupting her.

"He's a wonderful man," Molly replied. "We've known him since he was CEO of PayPal. He sent us that car for Christmas."

Sara was sitting next to Ben on the floor. She quietly put her hand on his to show her support as he tried to understand this truly insane day.

"And, of course, there's the Walmart stock," Molly continued. "Your grandfather Wallace started buying it when it first went public. The Wallace family and the Walton family consider themselves to be relatives, the good kind. I guess we have about $500 million of that."

There was silence in the room as Molly finished listing their stock holdings.

"Is that how you go permission for us to park the RV at the Walmart store in Springfield?" Holly asked.

"I called Jim Walton," Anderson replied. "Your granddad met his dad, Sam Walton, when they were just out of college. They both worked at J. C. Penny's in Des Moines. Who do you think buys all of our apples, and has for decades?"

"And now for Sara," Anderson continued.

Everyone's attention turned to her, although no one understood why she would be included.

"Sara, I think it is time to tell you a story about your family."

Sara looked very confused and tensed up with embarrassment.

"Sara, honey," Molly said, jumping into the conversation, "don't worry. It's a good story."

"Your grandfather," Anderson went on, "and I were great friends. Sara you were too young to know that, of course. When I told him we were going to invest in this new computer company, he handed me $1,000 in cash. He had just sold his crop and he asked me to invest it for his granddaughter, but not to tell her about it until she was 30 years old. He was a simple man who always said he didn't understand high finance, but he trusted Molly and me to do the right thing for his family.

"So, we bought Apple stock when it first went public," he continued, "and set up a separate account for his shares. It has been sitting at the brokers for all these years. I am happy to tell you that, as of tomorrow when you turn 30, it is your choice to have the stock transferred to you or, if you prefer, we can have it sold and you can have money."

Sara was on the brink of tears. This was coming at her without warning.

"By my figuring this morning," Anderson said, "your account is worth about $1.75 million."

CHAPTER 83

At that moment, Siobhan and Mackenzie returned home from Christmas shopping. Their arms were filled with packages. They were surprised to see all of Ben's family assembled in the living room for some sort of family gathering.

"Anyone hungry?" Anderson asked. "Siobhan, do you think you can get your steak house to take us a little earlier?"

"Mr. Wallace, for you, anything," she responded. "Let me make a quick phone call."

Less than a minute later, she said, "The table is ours whenever we get there, for as long as we want it. My close friends own the restaurant, and they know you are special guests."

"Wash up, children!" Molly said.

"We leave in fifteen minutes," Anderson announced. "And Siobhan, do you mind driving, too. Ben seems to have left his car behind where he used to work."

Siobhan nodded her agreement, although she didn't understand the sudden turn of events in Ben's career. Since it wasn't her place to ask, she just went with the flow.

CHAPTER 84

The Chef's Table at the Fulton Grille was hidden away in a special back room that was outfitted like a wine cellar, filled from floor to ceiling with the finest wines.

When Betty and Arnold Westwood arrived, they found seats of honor waiting for them next to Anderson and Molly.

"Let me introduce, Mr. and Mrs. Westwood," Anderson announced as he rose to his feet.

"Betty and Arnold, please," Betty interjected.

"Betty and Arnold, it is," Anderson continued. "They are Ben's new bosses for the next year while he learns their business. It's a very exciting day for us all and we are honored that you could join us tonight to celebrate.

"These are our children," Anderson went on. "Ben, of course, our daughter Holly and her husband, Todd, their two children, our grandchildren, Billy and Lily, our daughter, Caitlin, the children's part-time nanny, but really one of Wallaceton's finest grammar school teachers, Sara Holcolm, and Ben's roommates, Siobhan and Mackenzie. There you have it."

"On behalf of Arnold and myself," Betty began, "we are very pleased to meet you all and truly honored to be here to celebrate with you on the purchase of our company ... it is *yours* now," Betty looked at Anderson and winked, "and excited to begin the next chapters of our lives."

"Please join me in raising your glass of apple cider to toast and celebrate a new chapter for everyone here tonight!"

Anderson said.

"Merry Christmas!" Molly added.

Sara was sitting next to Ben at the opposite end of the table from his parents.

"Ben, this is some big day for you," Sara said to him softly.

Ben just rolled his eyes and nodded in agreement.

"You know," she went on, "Springfield is only a two-hour drive from Wallaceton. I have a really close friend from college who lives there. She has her own apartment. I could visit you and stay with her sometime. But only if you wanted me to."

Ben looked at Sara in a way he had never seen her before, and, for the first time, really realized the importance of hometown relationships and shared values.

"Sara, I would like that very much," he replied, and leaned over to meet her for a kiss.

THE END

About the Author

S. I. Wells moved to a small farm in southwest Iowa, known as flyover country, with his wife of 45 years, ten years ago. The farm has been in his family since the Civil War and has ancestral memories that mirror the history of the U.S.A. Not a farmer by profession, he lets his neighbors farm the acres in exchange for fresh vegetables and treats throughout the year.

He has a pig named Winston Churchill, a cow named Bessie, a wiener dog named Geronimo and a cat named Trouble.

After a varied career, he now devotes his days to writing heartfelt stories about ordinary people with strong values and grit who wind up overcoming the challenges life throws at them with dignity and grace.

Made in United States
North Haven, CT
28 November 2023

44706957R00126